The Waves

Jen Minkman

There once was a fairytale
about a strange man in the olden days
who could walk on water
and said he was sent by a God,
but we all know that is just make-believe
for children.
No one can walk on water,
that is why our Goddess will come for us by ship
when the time is right.

From the Annals of Praed the First,
one of the books in the Sanctuary of Our Lady
Annabelle

Prologue

THE FIRST memory I have of my grandfather is of a moment that we share together.

I'm sitting on his knee looking out over the harbor. Grandpa is smoking a pipe. He points at the horizon. "Look, Walt. Our ships are out there. And one day, another even more beautiful ship will appear at the horizon. A mighty ship to take us all away."

"Where to, Grandpa?" I ask curiously.

He remains quiet. "No one knows exactly," he says at last, "but that doesn't make it any less fantastic. One day, that ship will come in. And Annabelle will be on the prow with open arms, inviting us all to come on board."

The Goddess with black hair waving in the wind, as portrayed on the biggest wall of our temple.

"Why don't we sail to her ourselves?" I want to know.

"Because she promised she would come," Grandpa replies. "And in that promise we trust. It's only the Unbelievers who think they can do everything themselves. They have no faith in the Goddess."

I was only five, but I still clearly remember feeling a cold shiver running through my body after hearing that last remark. Most children in Hope Harbor are scared of the stories their parents tell them about the Unbelievers: if you don't visit the temple every week, they will get you in your sleep. If you don't listen to the priests, they will send you out into the wilderness behind the Wall where the Unbelievers dwell, their robes of black and masks of horror a sure sign of their sinfulness. Once they sink their claws into you, there's not a chance you will ever return.

But that was then.

I know better now – because I've been there, and yet I am still alive.

Part 1 - Ripples

1.

SHE MIGHT be gone, but I still know her.

"I remember my mother very clearly," I tell Yorrick, glaring at him with as much confidence as I can muster.

"I think you've just made it up," Yorrick assures me. He's my older, arrogant cousin. "You can't possibly remember how she sang for you. You were only *three*."

I'm sitting in the schoolyard eating an apple. Our classes have finished for the day, but Yorrick and I picked the school grounds to hang around and chat. His father won't be home anytime soon, anyway.

"How would you know?" I mumble around a bite of apple.

"I know more than you," Yorrick throws back. "I've already read ten books from my dad's library."

When Yorrick turns nineteen, he's supposed to have read them all. Which means he's in for quite a task in the year ahead, because the Bookkeeper's library contains thirty-four books in total. Once he has read them all, he's allowed to succeed his father as Bookkeeper of Hope Harbor.

I grumble inwardly, because Yorrick indeed knows more than I do. In fact, he knows more than everyone else our age. The education we get in school is mostly of a practical nature: how to repair houses and build new ones, construct a ship, grow vegetables and raise cattle. Of course, fishing skills are important too, and I've always found that more interesting than agriculture. Being able to find my own food in the wild gives me a sense of freedom and independence. Last year, I chose an elective about wild plants and berries. Apart from learning about survival, we study reading and writing, mathematics, and history mingled with religion. For us, the two go hand in hand. Nobody doubts Annabelle's love for us, nor the important part she has played – and will still play – in our history.

At times I wonder what kind of information can be found in my Uncle Nathan's library. The common people don't get to hear all of it. The Bookkeeper and the priests have exclusive access to the books, so I don't really know what kind of knowledge they contain.

"The books don't tell us about that sort of thing," I nevertheless protest. "They tell us how to make a living for ourselves so we'll be ready when Annabelle's Fleet arrives."

Yorrick spits in the sand. "Yeah, and you know what else they contain? Maps of the sea around Tresco. Detailing all the currents. And there's more."

I dazedly blink my eyes. I'm pretty sure Yorrick isn't supposed to tell me about this, but I don't care – his words have piqued my curiosity. "So what else?"

My cousin bends closer to me. "The Other Side," he whispers. "A different coastline than ours. And from the looks of it, it's not actually that far away."

That can't be right. The townspeople of Hope Harbor all know the sea is too vast to cross. Occasionally, we do sail out beyond our fishing waters, but those weekly trips are meant to welcome the Fleet in case it shows up at the horizon. We always need to be ready.

"That's impossible," I say decidedly. "The World across the Waters is way too far. If it were as close to Tresco as you're saying, someone would have sailed to the Other Side by now, right?"

Yorrick gives me a pondering look. "Well, maybe it's about time someone tried," he mumbles. "If you don't, you'll never find out."

Just then, the school's front door opens and out step three girls from the highest grade. Yorrick promptly sits up straight, rakes a hand through his brown hair and throws the girls his most winning smile. "Hello, ladies," he calls out ebulliently. "Any plans this afternoon?"

All three girls giggle. Yorrick is quite the charmer. Next to him, I always feel tongue-tied, but I do pay close attention to his way with girls whenever he's chatting with them and I'm just standing there like an idiot-sidekick. My older cousin is my biggest source of wisdom when it comes to situations like these.

"We're going to the beach," one of them announces. It's Alisa with her blonde curls. "Are you guys coming?"

Yorrick elbows me in the ribs. "She's inviting both of us, Walt. Come on, tag along."

My face fills with color. "I can't. I'm going to the temple with Grandpa Thomas this afternoon."

"Oh please. You go there every Friday. Can't you skip it for once?"

"No, actually, I can't."

Yorrick gets up. "Okay, your loss. I'm not saying no to three girls all to myself." He winks and waves at me before turning around and following Alisa and her friends down the road.

Actually, I would have liked to join them, but today is a special day. Exactly forty years ago, Grandpa lost his first fiancée to the Unbelievers, and we are commemorating that fact together in the temple today.

I leave the schoolyard and turn left. The road leading to the temple goes steeply uphill, and soon I feel parched. I take another apple out of my bag and eat the piece of fruit as I make my way toward Hope Harbor's sanctuary.

Annabelle's Temple is situated high atop Tresco's steep cliffs. The antechamber overlooks the wild, wide sea. When the temple holds silent services, the inner sanctum is never entirely quiet – you can always hear the seawind howling around the building, and if you are lucky enough to get into a deep trance, it's said that you can even hear Annabelle's voice on the wind.

Halfway through my ascent, I sit down on a bench at the side of the road, my gaze alighting on Hope Harbor below me. Hundreds of houses huddle together at the estuary of the river that originates in the mountains of Unbeliever territory and flows into the sea near our harbor. In the distance, I can see the green rooftop of Yorrick's house – the Bookkeeper's residence. My uncle governs our town, making sure no one is short of common commodities and everything runs like clockwork. People in our community contribute to tending the fires in the watchtowers, because most of us are scheduled for lighthouse shifts at least once a month. And all Hope Harborer with jobs remit part of their income to the temple so the priests can organize worship services for Annabelle and send ships containing votive offerings to her Realm.

Some gifts are also used to fund the building of new ships that will sail out to welcome her Fleet.

My father is superintendent to the shipbuilders. I've joined him on one of his welcoming ships sailing out when I was younger, but I turned out not to have his sea legs. In fact, I was pretty seasick. Maybe that was a slight disappointment to him, but he has never commented on it.

I squint my eyes at the horizon. Not too long ago, I firmly believed that the Fleet would one day appear at our shore, but lately, I've been wondering whether the story being told in the temple isn't just a sop to keep us happy. I don't discuss these worries with anyone: not with my dad and certainly not with Grandpa. Even Yorrick doesn't know I have my doubts.

Maybe we should just accept that this is our place in the world. Perhaps we are never meant to leave at all.

2.

WHEN I arrive at the temple court, a temple assistant in white robes is busy lighting the torches affixed to the marble pillars on opposite sides of the entrance. Tonight, more people will come, because Grandpa's private commemoration coincides with the celebration of summer. Many Hope Harborers will soon be here, wearing flowers in their hair and carrying blossom in baskets so they can welcome summer into our midst. They'll be expressing the hope that Annabelle will come this summer, taking us with her to the land no one has seen – the World across the Waters.

"Is my grandfather inside yet?" I ask him. Almost all the temple employees know him – Grandpa Thomas is a very religious man and he piously visits the temple every day.

"Yes, I saw him heading for the altar," the priest assistant nods with a smile.

Grandpa has just lit a big candle on the altar and is reverently staring at the flame chasing away the semi-darkness of the inner sanctum. When I approach him, he turns around and a smile lights up his face.

He extends his hand to me, and I take it and squeeze it for a second. "Hello, Grandpa."

"Hello, my boy," he replies. His eyes look wistful. In fact, as long as I can remember, grandfather has always had a certain air of sadness about him. That should be no surprise – his life hasn't been easy. His first, great love was taken from him by the Unbelievers, his wife left him after ten years of marriage, and his only daughter – my mother – passed away in the prime of her life. I know people who have lost their faith over less than that, and yet his trust in the Goddess has never once wavered. Or maybe it's because of this very burden that his faith is so strong: all we can do in the face of adversity is put our trust in a higher power and relinquish our worries, the high priests say.

Grandpa Thomas pulls me along to the bench we always use on this special day. It is in an alcove directly beneath a mural of Tresco. The western part of the island is full-color and features beautiful paintings of Annabelle and her daughters next to the dot on the map that is Hope Harbor. The eastern part of the island is empty and dark – it is the land behind the Wall where unbelief rules. The place where they took my grandfather's first love.

"Tell me about her," I say softly.

This is how we always start. I'll ask him that very question, so Grandpa can talk about how happy he and his fiancée were. Until one day, she didn't show up at the temple during an important holiday. He'll tell me how she disappeared from his life, having been kidnapped by the Unbelievers.

Only this time, my grandfather tells me a different story.

"Walt," he says with a weary voice, "I am going to tell you what I also told your mother when she turned sixteen. I want you to know how wrong it is to stray from our path."

"What do you mean?" I gaze at him warily.

"I want you to realize how dangerous the world on the other side of the island is. How important it is that we wait and put our trust and faith in the Goddess."

"But I know all that, Grandpa." Doesn't he remember what he did and didn't tell me before?

Grandpa slumps against the wall, staring unseeingly at the altar. On the rear wall is another, bigger mural of Annabelle, standing erect in a beautiful white boat decorated with yellow flowers, her black hair fluttering in the breeze.

And then, my grandfather speaks again. His voice is solemn and the first few words he utters are the same as always, but after that they are very different.

"Toja and I were happy together, until one day she didn't show up at the temple for the Spring Equinox. I was worried, as I had felt something was different about her behavior in the weeks leading up to spring."

I frown. "How?"

"She started to ask questions. About all kinds of things. She wanted to know how far away Annabelle's Realm was from ours. Why we couldn't go there. Why the priests said we had to wait. She even wanted to know what the Unbelievers looked like." His voice drops to a whisper. "She stopped going to the temple, Walt, because she thought the stories of the priests were nonsense."

"Are you serious?" I say hoarsely. His words startle me, and it's not just because he never told me this part of the story before – it's because I've been wondering about the validity of our legends myself.

"Yes, I am. And I know she reached a breaking point when I asked her to marry me. She was scared – poisoned with the thought that something better was waiting for us on the other side of the island. Annabelle was no longer the focus of her attention."

I let the silence stretch between us, looking at him expectantly. My grandpa takes a deep breath and puts his hand on my shoulder. "Toja was never abducted. She was curious. Curious enough to cross the Wall. But she never came back."

That evening, I come home late from roaming the streets without really taking notice of anything. The first time I pay attention to my surroundings again after hearing Grandpa's story, I find myself at the beach, but Yorrick is long gone and the sun has almost set. Dejectedly, I trudge to the harbor to stare at the boats floating on the water and the watchtowers lighting up the dusk with flaming fire.

So Grandpa's girlfriend had *chosen* to join the Unbelievers. She left him behind on purpose. Why?

The world on the other side of the Wall has always sort of fascinated me, but mostly because I wonder why the Unbelievers are so civil about staying on their side of Tresco. If they really are as bloodthirsty and dangerous as the priests would have us believe, why don't they ever attack? On the other hand, Toja never did come back. She went to have a look out of curiosity and that was the last time she was ever seen.

When I pass Yorrick's street, Alisa is just stepping out the front door of his house. She's smiling dreamily. Tomorrow I should ask Yorrick how their day on the beach went – from the looks of it, everything was smooth sailing.

"Hey, Walt," Alisa calls out to me when she spots me. "Going home?" She falls into step beside me.

"Yes, I am." I nod and fall silent again. Sometimes I hate myself, especially when feeling pressure to engage in small talk and failing miserably. We tacitly walk down the street. Alisa lives one block away, so we are headed in the same direction.

"How was the beach?" I finally manage to think up.

"Oh, it was lovely," Alisa exclaims. "We were sunbathing and watching the ships, and Yorrick bought us all cakes."

"But he only took *you* home," I state cleverly and look sideways to catch her eye. Hey, I just managed to make her blush. She's self-conscious about her friendship with my cousin. Feeling encouraged by the idea, I tease her a little bit more. "Did he have more cake for you at home, then?"

Alisa swivels around and gasps at me wide-eyed. "Walt! Don't say things like that! Before you know it, the entire town is going to talk about us." She gives a tiny shrug. "I mean... he *is* the Bookkeeper's son, you know. People watch his every move."

"So what," I say defiantly. "*He* invited you over, right? It's no one else's business."

Alisa smiles. "Does he ever talk about me?" she inquires, a little apprehensive tremor in her voice.

I shrug. "Sometimes."

"So what does he say?" she persists.

"You know… that he wants to wait for you after school." He didn't, not really, but I know for sure that he does.

Her face lights up. "Oh," she giggles.

Meanwhile, we've arrived at the corner of her street. "Say hi to Yorrick from me," she softly says before walking away with a spring in her step. "Faith and hope to you."

"Faith, hope and love," I reply. Looking at the way she walks away, I suddenly feel a bit jealous. I wish someone were that happy with attention from *me*.

"Where on earth have you been?" my father asks as soon as I cross the threshold.

"I was at the temple."

He frowns at me. "No, you weren't. That's where grandfather suggested I should look for you, so I did."

My face turns red. "Okay, I'm sorry. I just needed to think. Be on my own."

Dad sits back down at the kitchen table, rubbing his face wearily. "Why did you feel the need to lie about that? What have they told you at the temple that caused you to get upset and wander about town for hours?"

I sit down with a puzzled face. Never in my life have I heard my dad criticize the temple, but he undoubtedly sounds like he's blaming them for something now. "Dad, what's wrong?"

He remains silent, fumbling with the mug of milk in his hands. Two plates of meat and vegetables are sitting on the table next to his mug – one of them still full and one of them half-empty. He must have waited for me to come home for dinner, but I never showed.

"I just wanted for you to find your own way, Walt," he says at last, sounding tired. "That's what I've always hoped for."

"But you don't agree with the path I've chosen?" I ask sullenly.

A smile flits across his face. "I think you're a very sensible boy. You do well in school, you don't get into trouble and you have the right kind of friends. You help your grandpa whenever he needs you."

Again he pauses, which causes me to sigh with impatience. "Dad? I can take it."

"Grandpa has always pushed your mother into one direction when she was young," my dad continues. "Because of what Toja had done, he made sure your grandma and mother wouldn't do the same. He'd flip out whenever they so much as *looked* in the direction of the Wall. Frankly I'm not surprised your grandmother decided to leave him. Grandpa simply never got over the loss of his fiancée. Even today he still commemorates her disappearance."

I bite my lip. The way Dad makes it sound, it seems kind of stupid. It's as if Grandpa is still living in the past.

"I didn't want to raise you the way he raised your mother," my father concludes. "I just wanted

21

you to be you and let you make your own choices. I told Grandpa Thomas he shouldn't force you into anything. But lately, you've been spending so... so much time in that temple."

I nod, looking at him in anticipation.

With a jerk he pushes his chair back and gets up. "I don't want you to visit the place anymore, not anytime soon." Before I can even utter another word to protest, he whirls around and barges out of the kitchen.

***

That night, I dream about Mom. I'm just as old as I am now, but somehow I am holding her hand like a little kid as we walk down the street together. I feel young, small and afraid. The streets abound with people holding torches, trying to scare away the darkness. It is a pitch-black night and there is no moon, and yet I can see my mother's face very clearly in the dream.

"What's going on?" I ask anxiously. "Where are all those people going?"

My mother smiles. "To the ship of gold, Walt. We sail tonight. We're leaving."

"Going where?" I don't like the look in her eyes – she's glancing past me to a place I can't reach.

"Away from here. To Annabelle."

Suddenly, my father is standing in front of us with tears in his eyes. "Please, stay with us," he begs, grabbing my mother's shoulders.

She is still smiling. Her eyes are full of emptiness. "I have to go."

"Mom!" I scream when she pulls herself from his grasp and breaks into a run down the street, toward the harbor. I see a sea of people bleeding into the deep.

When I wake up, I no longer remember what her face looked like.

3.

"WALT! YOU want some honey cake?"

Samuel nudges me in the side. We're in line at the bakery stall and it's nearly our turn, but I'm preoccupied with something else besides lunch. Squinting my eyes, I peer at the other side of the market square. I thought I saw her.

"Uhm, yes, why not," I mumble absently. "And Yorrick wants a salty pretzel."

Yes, it's really her. Her white-gray hair is pinned up in a neat bun. It used to be white-blonde, like mine, but I have seen it turn gray from a distance over the years.

Grandma. My mom's mom.

Dad claims Mom looked a lot like her, but I can't imagine that. Whenever I think of my mother, I remember warmth, a gentle and sweet voice, and a sense of security. When I look at this woman, I see a wall of ice that has blocked the few attempts I've made at contact. She seems so old and unapproachable.

"Are you coming or what?" Samuel is starting to sound impatient. He grabs my arm, but I pull loose.

"I have to do something. Why don't you and Yorrick go to the park now? I'll catch up with you guys later."

Without looking back, I cross the square, heading straight for her without breaking stride. I don't slow down when I see her eyes widen in surprise, her mouth setting into a grim line.

"Hello, Grandma," I say, keeping the tremor running through my entire body out of my voice. "How are you these days?"

"I'm fine." Her gaze wanders over my face and her eyes soften. "And how about you, Walt? How old are you now?"

"Fifteen. And quite frankly, I'm not doing too well."

"What's wrong?" She takes a step closer to me. "Trouble at home?"

Why would she say that? Is that the first thing coming to mind when she thinks of Dad and Grandpa? Maybe I shouldn't have done this. Still, my curiosity outweighs my anxiety.

"Do you have time to go and have tea somewhere? Can we... talk about Mom, maybe?"

She nods, pointing at the entrance to an alley behind the vegetable stall. "Why don't you follow me? I live close by."

She's inviting me to come to her house. Her armor of ice is suddenly showing cracks. And now what? I don't even know where she lives, let alone with whom. Maybe I have a whole bunch of half-cousins I don't know anything about.

The narrow street runs into a circular square lined by seven houses. My grandma heads for a house with a red door and white flowers on the windowsills on either side of the entrance.

It smells good when I step inside, a scent of freshly-baked cookies still lingering in the air. Somehow, it stirs my memories of a time when I still had parents, when Mom would take care of me and Yorrick when our dads were at work. Deep in thought, I close my eyes and breathe in the scent that seems so familiar.

"What is that song you're singing?" a voice interrupts my reverie. I whip around and see how pale my grandmother has become. She's dropped her bag of groceries, spilling apples all over the floor.

"I... I don't know," I stammer. "Was I humming something?"

She nods, tears welling up in her eyes. "That's your mother's song. You still remember that?"

A smile spreads across my face. The song I sometimes wake up with after it's haunted my dreams all night... it really *is* my mother's voice I'm hearing. Yorrick can say whatever he likes – I know what she used to sound like. I remember.

When my grandmother bends down to pick up her fruit and vegetables from the floor, I stop her. "I'll take care of that, Grandma. Why don't you make us a cup of tea? And I'd love one of your cookies to go with it."

She laughs. "It's a family recipe. Sara used to bake them for you all the time."

While I'm busy clearing the floor, my grandma makes tea in the kitchen, humming the same tune I was singing. It's strange, but I feel at home here. I should have done this a long time ago.

A while later Grandma puts a tray with tea and cookies on the table. She smiles at me, but her voice is serious when she asks me: "What is it you want to talk about, Walt?"

I keep quiet for a long time. "I would really like to know why you don't want anything to do with us," I say at last, sadness evident in my voice. "I mean, I completely understand why you don't want to see Grandpa anymore. The two of you are divorced, and you can't really stay friends after breaking up." That last bit is not actually me. It's something I heard Yorrick say one time, but hey – I want to sound grown-up and knowledgeable.

Grandma sips from her tea and lets her gaze wander to the mantel shelf. "Do you remember what your mother looked like, Walt?" She points at a painting hanging on the wall above it. With a lump in my throat, I stare at the portrait. She has blue eyes and blonde hair, just like me. Did she look the same in my dream? I don't know. Somehow, my memories mainly consist of emotions – what it felt like to hear her voice, what it was like when she held me. We don't have any pictures of her. And now I'm wondering why, if Grandma does have one.

She seems to guess what thought crosses my mind. "I believe your father removed all images of Sara from the house after she died, because he was too sad. And because he was blaming himself."

"Why would he blame himself?" I look at her in confusion. "Didn't she die of a sickness?"

Grandma takes a deep breath. "Is that the story Thomas has told you?" A bitter laugh escapes her throat. Her teacup clatters in its saucer.

A coldness seeps into my limbs. "Can you tell me what really happened?" I ask apprehensively.

"Why I'm avoiding your family goes a long way back. When I married Thomas, he'd been alone for two years after Toja's disappearance. I was an acquaintance of him for a long time and we became close friends. Over time, we grew even closer. When he proposed to me, I was over the moon. I was aware that he still thought about Toja a lot, but I didn't think it was important as long as he loved me too."

"Didn't he love you then?"

She heaves a heavy sigh. "In his way he did, I think. It just wasn't enough for me. I couldn't compete with a woman from his past who wasn't even around anymore. On top of that, his constant dread of whatever was lurking beyond the Wall didn't really help either. So after ten years, I gave up.

Sara was nine at the time. Thomas did everything in his power to make sure she chose him to live with, and when she grew older, she felt more attached to him than to me, even despite my best efforts. Why exactly, I don't really know. She may have felt pity for her father – he'd been twice abandoned by a woman he loved and didn't want to lose the only daughter he had."

I gulp something down. "But he did lose her."

"Yes, he did, and I will always blame *him* for that. I wanted to show Sara there was a life beyond the temple, but he wouldn't let me. He started to restrict visits to our daughter, and he didn't want me to see you at all. And your dad never spoke out against it – he blindly chose Thomas's side."

"So what did my grandpa say to her about the temple, exactly?" I ask, remembering my dad mentioning the same thing last night, too.

"Thomas was simply obsessed with the idea that we should shape our lives around Annabelle's Arrival, and it carried over into Sara's life. Up until the point where she lost all sense of reality and joined the Sect of the Golden Ship."

I blink at her dumbly. A golden ship like the one in my nightmare? That's odd. I never heard of a temple denomination going by that name before today. I shoot my grandmother a quizzical look.

She shakes her head, her face bleak. "No, Walt, that was before your time. The sect no longer exists.

It's because they believed Annabelle was waiting for us in the afterlife, and lingering in this one was unnecessary and troublesome."

The afterlife. Her words punch me in the gut, making me feel sick to my stomach. "Are you saying she…" I falter.

Grandma nods. "They committed suicide. Collectively. So their ship of gold would take them to the Other Side without delay."

When I emerge from the house, the wind has picked up. The air smells tangy with salt. Gigantic clouds drift across the sky, blotting out the sun. The air is as dark as my heart.

So this is why Dad suddenly wants to keep me away from the temple. He's afraid history will repeat itself. Of course the Sect of the Golden Ship doesn't exist anymore, but my frequent visits to our sanctuary certainly bother him. Grandpa, however, sees no harm in me joining him for temple services. Perhaps he saw no harm in my mother joining the sect either.

The last thing my grandmother said still sings around in my head. When she embraced me at the door and told me I shouldn't hesitate to visit again, I'd asked her if it was best to keep my mouth shut to Grandpa about this afternoon.

"Beware of him. In his world, nothing is ever his fault," she'd replied.

4.

"WHERE THE heck have you been, man?" Yorrick moves aside so I can sit down next to him on 'our' bench in the park. "Samuel said you left the market on some urgent business?"

I give a tiny shrug. Yorrick will hear the story about my grandma at some point, but not here and not now – it's too personal for that. Samuel is here too. A little ways away from us, I can see Alisa and her friends sitting on the lawn, giggling every time they look our way. "Yeah. Something like that."

Samuel follows my gaze and elbows Yorrick. "How's your girlfriend, then?" he asks eagerly.

My cousin starts to smile broadly. "Just fine. She came round my house last night, you know, just for a little bit." He winks at Sam, who shoots him an equally wide grin back. They exchange one of those glances that make me feel like I'm just a little boy compared to them, and I hate it. This is the reason I don't like hanging out with Yorrick and Samuel both – I feel like an outsider. When it's just me and my cousin, it's still clear he's older and tougher than me, but I also feel a connection with him.

Samuel hands me my honey cake, which has turned all soggy in the heat. The first bite is too sticky in my mouth, so I put the rest aside and flop down in the grass to stare up at the sky.

Clouds chase past me in the blustery breeze. Seagulls turn lazy arcs overhead and disappear toward the horizon.

They don't know how lucky they are.

"Are you off *again*?" Samuel asks in surprise when I get up from the ground. "Stick around, man. The girls are just coming our way."

I shake my head. "I want to take a walk. I'll see you guys later." Yorrick raises an eyebrow at me before I turn around and exit the park.

The road I follow takes me to the edge of Hope Harbor, to the town section of the farmers and hunters who provide us with wheat and vegetables from the fields and game from the woods.

And then, I leave town altogether, disappearing under the trees of the forest. It is much cooler under the canopy of branches and leaves. The suddenly fresh air gives me goosebumps. The forest trail climbs up precipitously and the loose sand on the track tires my feet, but I plow doggedly on. After a walk of about one hour, the road ends. A narrow track used only sporadically continues between the trees. And still, I walk on. Only now is it beginning to dawn on me that I didn't exactly prepare well for this trip. My stomach is starting to rumble and my mouth is dry with thirst. When I come to a halt, I listen carefully in the hopes of hearing running water over the rushing of blood in my ears. The river should be close.

And indeed, I can hear water somewhere. I change course and turn left, making my way around high shrubs and old oaks until I end up at a brook – a small distributary of the river. I dip my hands in, cup them and eagerly gulp down some of the water coursing past my feet on its way to the sea. Hidden under a large rock I discover some edible roots that I dig out and wash so I can eat them later. First and foremost, I want to reach my goal.

After another hour of walking, I'm here. I'm right in front of the Wall.

I've only been here once before, when Grandpa Thomas took me to see this place and warn me. In my memory, the Wall was higher and the stones were darker and more sinister-looking. Now that I am older and taller, the separation between us and the Unbelievers doesn't seem that high and solid anymore. Hardly enough to stop people if they wanted to cross. I could hop over myself if I could find a tree close enough to the Wall to climb over…

Why am I even thinking about that? What could possibly be waiting for me on the other side? Nothing. And yet, I walked all this way so I could see what the place looks like. Now that I know that at least one person from Hope Harbor has crossed this barrier of her own free will, this Wall is calling to me as if I'm attached to it by invisible string. Would my mom have ventured out here too, if Grandpa hadn't tried so hard to keep her away?

All of a sudden, I feel angry with her. She left me and took the easy way out. If only she'd taken me and crossed this Wall instead of the great divide between life and death, she would still be with me today. My foot kicks against the brick angrily, and I sag down with my back against the Wall. Gray sky peeks through the branches above my head. The air in the forest now feels muggy, which is a bad sign. It wouldn't surprise me if a thunderstorm erupted soon – unfortunately, I still have to make it back home, which will take me at least two hours.

Right at that moment, I can hear a sound on the other side of the Wall. Some sort of rustling in the undergrowth, like the sound of someone walking there. My heart speeds up and I scramble to my feet without making a sound. I *have* to know what's on the other side. Suddenly, I don't care if there are Unbelievers walking around there who could see me. My own world feels too small, too stifling, due to all the half-truths I've been told.

I start following the stone barrier. Unfortunately, I don't see any trees close enough to scale and easily cross the Wall, but I do spot a few crumbled holes in the surface resembling hand- and footholds to use for climbing. My heart hammering in my throat, I put

34

one foot in the lowest hole and haul myself up by using the other holes above my head. The Wall is thick; despite some stones having crumbled away, none of the holes I'm using can be used as peep-holes to show me what's on the other side. With trembling arms, I pull myself all the way up and balance at the top of the barrier, one foot almost slipping from the highest, shallowest hole.

My head pops up over the edge. This is it: I am looking at the other side of the Wall.

It looks disappointingly the same as our side. Trees as far as the eye can see. Green and bushes and brown earth and fallen leaves. No ferocious armies in black robes, no monsters or any of the other things our parents used to terrify us with when we were children.

A movement in the brushwood draws my attention. I hear the same rustling sound as I did before. And as I peer down intently, a sheep emerges from the bushes. The animal bleats plaintively and looks at me with startled eyes – it looks even more lost than I feel.

"Hey there," I say gently. "Come-come-come." I have no idea how to coo at a sheep, to be honest – my visits to the farm can be counted on one hand. "Come here, uhm... Fluffy?"

The Unbelieving sheep stares at me suspiciously. It's a surprise it's not actually a *black* sheep. An involuntary giggle rises up in me due to my nerves and my own insipid joke, which seems to be Fluffy's cue to take off. The animal pivots around and hobbles away. Just before it disappears into the bushes, though, my gaze alights on a large, red stain on its rearside.

Fluffy is marked. This sheep belongs to someone.

5.

THE SUN has already set when I finally arrive home. My dad is sitting at the table together with Grandpa, his face like thunder.

"Where did you go *this* time?" he snarls.

"William." My grandpa tries to appease him, putting a hand on my fathers's arm.

Dad impatiently swats him away. "No, don't. I have a right to know where my son was."

"I was with Yorrick…" I start out.

He glares at me. "Please, spare me your lies. I was worried sick. Yorrick was here to pick you up for your lighthouse shift and he told me you'd taken off for a stroll all by yourself this afternoon. He had no idea where you could be."

Oh no. Our watchtower shift together – I completely forgot. Yorrick and I were supposed to man the left tower tonight. My cousin is probably livid.

"I'm going to the harbor," I say, walking to the kitchen top to grab some fruit.

"You're not going anywhere until you tell me where you were," my father snaps.

Suddenly, something collapses inside of me. "I went to the Wall," I blurt out in a rage. "I climbed all the way to the top and I saw the other side. And it's not all as scary as it's made out to be, trust me." I look at my grandfather defiantly.

Grandpa Thomas pales. "You... you've been to the other side?"

I snort. "No. I just looked. All I saw was a lost sheep." The fact I also saw clear evidence of civilization is best left out for now. "Oh, and by the way, do you know where I was *before* I went to the Wall? At Grandma's. And she told me about Mom. She didn't die of a disease, did she? She was driven straight into the arms of a suicide sect." I look at Grandpa Thomas. "Because you wanted her to be as pious as possible, and you..." I turn to Dad. "You were too blind to see what was wrong with her. So don't you talk to *me* about lies!" If looks could kill, the two men at the table would now wither away.

"Walt, I..." Dad looks at me helplessly. Grandpa has averted his eyes and is staring out the window, his jaw working.

"Don't know what to say?" I finish for him. "Well, better keep your mouth shut then. I'm going to the harbor. Have a splendid night together, you two."

With tears of anger welling up in my eyes, I barrel out the door. I'm completely out of breath when I arrive at the harbor after only five minutes, starting up the narrow path leading up to the left watchtower. The fire up there burns peacefully, but the fire in my heart is starting to consume me from the inside. I have to talk to Yorrick.

"Sit down." Yorrick points at a stool in the corner of the tower room when I get to the upstairs floor. "I'm half-tempted to tie you to your chair so you won't run out of here again." He sounds gruff, but his brown eyes sparkle good-humoredly.

I exhale loudly. "Yeah, yeah, I know. I'm late and I'm acting strange. But that's because my *life* is strange."

My cousin gives me a searching look, and that's when I spill everything to him about how my life was turned upside down in the past few days – Grandpa's confession about Toja, Dad's warning about the temple, Grandma's revelation about my mother's death... ripples on a sea that used to be calm and smooth. Black waves swelling and threatening to pull me under.

"Now I understand why my parents never want to talk about Aunt Sara." Yorrick sounds upset. "Were you at your grandmother's to talk about this all night?"

I shake my head. "I went up to the Wall."

"You *what*?"

"I don't know. Maybe because I think they've told us lies about that as well."

Yorrick nods slowly, pulling a case of cigarettes from his pocket. He always rolls some before we come here on our shifts. I stoke the fire in the pit and then hand over the hot poker to Yorrick so he can light cigarettes for the two of us. He gives me the slimmest one from the case, so the tobacco won't be too heavy for me.

We sit quietly shoulder to shoulder smoking our cigarettes. At last, Yorrick clears his throat. "I also want to know the truth," he says quietly. "I've been reading things, Walt. There's more to know about the Other Side than the common people here are aware of."

"What kinds of things?"

Yorrick rubs his forehead. "There are maps. Maps from a time *before* our history. Our island apparently used to consist of several smaller islands. They were called the Scilly Isles. It was not until massive earthquakes caused the seabed to rise that they became one, in the era of our ancestors. And this one island isn't that far away from the Other Side."

He pulls a black crayon from his pocket and gets up from his stool. I watch Yorrick use the seat to draw six jagged shapes, putting names next to each of them. "Tresco," I mumble. Our own island. "Bryher. Samson. St Martin. St Agnes. St Mary." I blink my eyes in disbelief at the islands, because they all bear names I've known since childhood.

Yorrick nods. "That's right. Agnes and Mary – Annabelle's daughters. Martin – Annabelle's partner. And of course we know those other names too."

Samson's Cliffs. Bryher Beach. "Were the islands named after the daughters of the Goddess?" I ask uncertainly.

The silence stretches. Yorrick wipes out his drawing and takes a long drag of his cigarette. "I don't know," he speaks up at last. "Were the places on our island named after the gods, or were the gods named after the old places?"

"Good Goddess, Yorrick," I whisper fiercely. "That map discredits the entire religious theory as avowed by the three high priests! And what about their claim that our island is the only one in the world? That there's nothing beyond it that we can see? That the Other Side is so far away only Annabelle can make the journey?" I fire off one question after another.

"What's even more intriguing is that my father *knows* about this and chooses to keep quiet," Yorrick quietly adds. "He's been Bookkeeper for all these years, but he has never once publicly called the priests' words into question – never demanded more people should know about this."

I heave a deep sigh. "Yorrick, what exactly have you discovered about Annabelle's Realm?"

"I don't even know if there *is* such a thing, Walt."

I frown. "But you said the Other Side was closer than we've always believed."

Yorrick stubs out his cigarette. "I saw a coastline on the map. According to the old books, the region is called Cornwall. I have no clue whether Annabelle lives there or not, but I intend to find out."

He stares at me silently. Slowly but surely, the meaning of his words sinks in. "You want to actually go there," I say flatly.

"Yes. The minute I succeed my father as Bookkeeper, I'm assembling a team to build the largest ship ever to sail past the horizon. Everybody should contribute. I'm going to ask your father to help me design it. We have a right to finally know what's waiting for us out there. What was promised to us."

"But what about the priests?"

Yorrick laughs derisively. "The priests don't rule Hope Harbor, Walt – our family does. If they insist on keeping everyone in the dark about things and shying away from learning new things, that's their problem. But I'm not going to help them do it. Under my rule, we'll see the dawn of a new age."

In a soft but resolute voice, Yorrick continues to lay out his plans. He wants to arrange a meeting with the high priests as soon as possible. He wants to take Finn, the youngest priest, on board his ship as an emissary. He has even come up with a name for the ship: it should be called the *Explorer*. The crew should consist of men and women of all different kinds of trades.

I can't focus on his story completely, because something's bothering me. Even though Yorrick's enthusiasm should be infectious, I can't ignore one very important question playing through my mind.

If the World across the Waters is really as close as Yorrick claims, why has no one ever come to *us*?

I'm not so sure I really believe in the land of Cornwall.

I'm not sure of anything anymore.

I think I've turned into an Unbeliever.

6.

IN THE days following my outburst, the atmosphere at home is so tense I could cut it with a knife. My father and grandfather don't mention the things I've said to them anymore, but they also don't apologize for the things they have kept from me. That's why I don't speak to either of them whenever we are all at home.

After school, I tag along with Yorrick and Alisa, who are going steady now, and sometimes I visit my grandma. I love listening to the stories she tells me about my mother, even if I still feel sad and sometimes angry when I think of her. She may have loved me, but she still decided to leave me. Maybe if my grandpa and grandma hadn't separated, my life would look very different today.

One evening, Yorrick shows up at my door unannounced. Surprised, I let him in and we go outside to sit in the garden. "I thought you had plans for a romantic dinner with Alisa tonight?" I say.

"She didn't feel well. And I actually really wanted to talk to you, Walt. Shall we go to the cliffs?"

That's the place we used to go kiting when we were kids. There's a coastal path running on top of the Samson Cliffs with a magnificent view of the sea, and the wind never lets up. Yorrick has picked this path to go jogging every day – something he's been doing for years now to keep in shape. Sometimes I join him, but I prefer running on the safe streets of Hope Harbor. The unpredictable blasts of wind at Samson make it dangerous to walk too close to the edge. Yorrick is a person who likes to seek out danger, but I'm definitely not. After all, what good is it to be in good shape if you take a plunge down the cliffs?

Yorrick leads the way as we jog up the coastal path. The first stretch cuts through a patch of woodland and is so narrow we can't run next to each other, but once we reach the top of the cliffs and break out of the woods, he slows down and I catch up with him.

"It's happening tomorrow morning," he tells me with a tremor in his voice. "There's a meeting at the temple and I'm going to tell the priests about my plans. I can't wait to hear what they will think."

"Well, they won't be chomping at the bit to let you build a ship," I reply. "I bet they want to talk you out of it – they'll reason it's only going to cause unrest among the Hope Harborers. It will distract their flock from faith and hope."

Yorrick sits down on a rock and exhales in agitation. "Yes, that's what my father told me as well."

"Oh? You told him about your plans?"

"No, I didn't mention them. Frankly, I want to keep them to myself for the time being. I didn't tell anyone except you. All I did was ask him why we've never tried to reach the Other Side. I told him I had seen the maps."

"So how did he respond?" I can't help but smile, feeling flattered that Yorrick has chosen *me* to share his plans with. All of a sudden, I don't feel like an insignificant, fifteen-year-old boy anymore. I am worthy enough to share knowledge with – I'm the Bookkeeper's nephew. And best friend to the future ruler of our town.

Yorrick frowns. "Allegedly, some eighty years ago a ship sailed out toward Cornwall, but it never returned. After that one attempt, no one else has ventured out."

I swallow down the lump suddenly lodged in my throat. I knew it – there is nothing. There is no Other Side. That's why we are here all alone, waiting for something that will most likely never come. Coldness creeps into my heart when I think of what it would be like to spend the rest of my life here, convinced there is no Other Side. I don't believe in it anymore. The thought of staying here is suffocating me – I'll be an Unbeliever amongst Hope Harborers of good faith.

I'd rather die aboard a ship that has at least *tried* to get out of here.

"Promise me one thing," I say gravely. "When you leave for the Other Side, take me with you."

Yorrick smiles. "Of course. Why not? It's time for us to see the whole wide world."

We get up and pick our way back down the path. The wind is howling around us. My cousin tells me how he wants to approach my father, organize a competition for our best shipbuilders to design a three-master – something we have never done before. There was never any need, because we don't sail too far away. He wants to think big and involve the entire population of Hope Harbor. The enthusiasm in his voice is no longer infectious; all it does is make me sad. The fact that I've lost faith in Annabelle's Realm is eating away at me – I *want* to believe, but I can't.

"Shall we meet at the cliffs again tomorrow afternoon?" Yorrick proposes when we're back at my house after our evening stroll. "I'm going for a run at three o'clock. If you meet me at half past three, I'll be done exercising so I can tell you all about the meeting."

In the distance, the clock strikes ten. I had a lesson about that clock in the tower not too long ago – apparently, the timepiece has always been there and the current Timekeeper is a direct descendant of the very first man who operated it. Every month, it needs to be wound up by using a crank. The weights have been replaced a number of times. The clock was given to us by Annabelle so we can count the hours we've been waiting for her appearance.

So far, one-hundred and fifty years have tick-tocked away.

Once more, I feel a wave of despondency wash over me. How many more years will be added to that number, years in which we will all fruitlessly wait for our Goddess?

"Yeah, let's do that," I reply. "I'll see you tomorrow."

When I enter the house, my father is in the kitchen cutting vegetables. He turns around and takes a step toward me. "Walt, we need to talk." He puts the knife and the carrots down. "Look, I'm sorry I lied to you."

I give a surly nod. Okay, he apologized. Maybe I should extend an olive branch. "Apology accepted. What do you want to talk about?"

We sit down at the table. Dad sighs deeply and puts his hand on mine. "I never meant to hurt you," he starts. "I thought it would be easier for you to believe your mother had died from an illness, so you wouldn't think she abandoned you. Because it is that very thought that plagued me for years afterward. I blamed myself for what happened, but I also blamed her."

I bite my lip when I see tears well up in his eyes. "Could you have done anything differently?" I ask, my voice strangled.

"I still wonder sometimes." Dad shakes his head. "Your mother was depressed. She wasn't very stable after you were born, and the only thing that seemed to still cheer her up was visiting the temple. Of course, Grandpa was all in favor of it; he said it would strengthen her faith. But I had my doubts – I wanted her to talk to *me* about her confusion. About the meaning of life on this island."

"So what *is* the meaning of life on this island?" I ask sharply. "Waiting? Sitting around being vigilant?"

He shrugs. "Walt, I don't know. Maybe there is nothing. Or maybe there's something waiting for us across the Waters and we should go to it if it doesn't come to us. Maybe there's a world on the other side of the Wall that is better than ours. I honestly don't know, and I wish I could tell you something better, but I can't."

"No, Dad, it's okay." I pat his hand. "I'm past the age I believe you know everything, you know."

He stifles a laugh and looks at me wistfully. "You've grown up so fast," he says, his voice full of sudden wonder. "And you're wise for your age. I'm proud you're my son. And you know what: I'm not going to tell you what to do and what not to do. Not anymore. If it makes you happy to trudge all the way to the Wall every day, stare at it or even hop over it, go right ahead. It's something you'll have to figure out for yourself. You want to visit the temple every day? That should be your choice. It's your life."

I shake my head. "I don't think I'll be visiting the temple anytime soon."

"That will upset Grandpa Thomas."

"Yes, I know. But, like you said, it's my life, not his."

We stare at each other silently. I wish I could tell him more about my life – about Yorrick's plan, or about that marked sheep I saw in Unbeliever Territory – but at the same time, I want to keep those things to myself for a little while longer. As it is, I'm just glad we're not fighting anymore.

"I'm going to bed." I have to get up early for school tomorrow.

"I think I'll turn in for the night as well."

We simultaneously get up and blow out the candles in the kitchen, leaving one on to put inside the lantern. I carry it upstairs when we go up to the second floor.

Passing my grandfather's bedroom, I can't help but notice his light is still on.

"Grandpa?" I knock lightly.

"Yes, my boy?"

I cross the threshold and take a deep breath. "I'm here to tell you I don't want to go to the temple anymore. For a while, anyway."

He silently observes me. Then he nods. "I hope you will find back your faith, Walt," he softly says. "I took you to Annabelle's temple under my supervision. I have never let you stray from my sight. I wanted to take good care of you after what happened to your mother."

As I listen to him, the anger drains from my body. I don't agree with the way Grandpa Thomas handled things, but I know he meant well. Now the time has come for him to let me go, and he's trying to. He doesn't attempt to convince me I'm wrong, although it's clear he thinks I'm lost.

"Thank you, Grandpa," I reply. "For everything."

That night, I sleep peacefully and without any nightmares.

7.

I GET up at the break of day. Before I go to school, I want to visit the temple one last time. With my schoolbag dangling from my shoulder, I follow the road upward.

The sun has just come up behind me, its rays turning the sea into a sparkling, shimmering world of red and gold. A world of water as far as the eye can see.

Before I know it, I'm in front of the temple building. The door is open, as always, and I head straight for the altar. The familiar mural of Annabelle stares down at me from the rear wall of the temple. Her blue eyes are friendly and inviting, her black hair dancing in the breeze like the waves of the endless sea. To her right is a smaller boat carrying her two daughters, Mary and Agnes. To her left is Martin, her lover, standing on the beach.

"Where are you?" I softly whisper as I gaze at the painting. "Why won't you come? Are you really out there somewhere?"

Of course she doesn't reply. My heart feels empty. I can't rely on her anymore, no matter how much I wish I still could.

I am sure of it now: I'm done here. My place is on a ship that will sail far away from this place.

On my way down, I bump into Yorrick as the clock in the tower just strikes eight. It's clear my cousin wants to take his time to talk to the three priests, because they don't usually come to the temple for services at this hour. This means an early start for them today.

I raise my hand in passing. "I'll see you this afternoon," I say with a smile. "Good luck."

The day seems to drag on forever, mostly due to the fact I'm just dying to know how Yorrick's meeting went. For a moment, I'm toying with the idea of skipping my final class of the day, but that happens to be History and I flunked my last two tests.

The teacher reads from his textbook in a droning voice and turns around to the blackboard to write down some questions for us to ponder. I stare at the board with an unseeing gaze, the letters dancing in front of my eyes. Quite frankly, I have no idea what the man is on about, so I jump in my seat when he suddenly turns his attention to me.

"What do *you* think of this particular question, Walt?" he booms, his piercing gaze landing on me.

"Uhm..." I scratch my head. "Which question would that be, sir?"

He taps on the board, an annoyed frown creasing his eyebrows. "The question about the Unbelievers.

Should we plead for Annabelle to visit them as well when she arrives, or have they missed the boat, so to speak?"

I stare down at my hands, a contemptuous smile tugging at my lips. This man doesn't understand. *Nobody* understands. "I don't think Annabelle will ever get here, sir," I mumble. "So we can't ask her anything either, can we?"

A heavy silence descends on the classroom.

"I'm sorry, *what* was that?" the history teacher snaps.

I look up, meeting his disapproving gaze without shame. "I think we are waiting in vain," I say loud and clear. "How do we know she exists? How do we know her name? Because she's not in the books, you know. Only her daughters are in there, and they're not even goddesses in those accounts."

I realize too late that I've said too much. Yorrick shared that information with me, but that doesn't mean I should blaze it abroad to everyone else.

Fortunately, the teacher is too angry with me to recognize the fact that I'm putting forward some really strange ideas. His face turns red with anger as he points an accusatory finger at me. "How we know her name? The first Bookkeeper knew she would come, and he has waited till the end of his days for her. Do you doubt the words of our first ruler?"

My chair legs scrape the floor when I impatiently push my seat back. I get up and raise my chin. "I won't tolerate you speaking to me like that," I snap back equally angry. "I'm the Bookkeeper's nephew. Who the heck do you think you are?"

The teacher visibly pales at my words. "Maybe you should see the nurse," he fumbles. "You're confused. You don't know what you're saying."

"Yes, maybe I should." I snatch up my bag and stomp out of the classroom. Instead of turning left to the nurse's station, though, I go right and step outside so I can cool off in the schoolyard.

I wantonly kick a pebble into the gutter. Why should I stick around, actually? Of course the teacher will want to talk to me after class, but the last thing I want today is detention. He can wait until tomorrow. It's a much better idea to head for the cliffs, so I can talk to Yorrick sooner.

The strong winds of early morning have died down a bit. The first part of my walk uphill takes me past the temple. As I turn left at the fork in the road to take the coastal path to the cliffs, the sun breaks through the clouds. Rays of sunlight illuminate the seawater here and there. The sea looks gray and dark today. Despite the fact that it is now officially summer, I'm not impressed with the temperatures yet. Only a few more weeks and school will be out for summer break. It would be nice if we could actually swim in the sea without freezing our hands and feet off. I'm looking forward to my vacation – Yorrick and Alisa said they were planning on staying in Uncle Nathan's beach hut for a few weeks, which means parties and Yorrick acting as my official matchmaker. He's been trying to hook me up with a girl for a while now, but my lack of confidence has stopped me from really going along with it so far.

The shadow of a smile tugs at my mouth. Lately, I've felt confused, but I feel stronger at the same time. What I said to the teacher about me being the Bookkeeper's nephew worked better than I'd expected – he was shitting bricks, I could tell. I have quite some clout within this community, and I decide that this will be my summer. It's time to come out of my shell.

Far away in town, the clock strikes three. I'm too early. Yorrick is probably still doing his warm-up. Oh well, no problem – I'll wait. I'd rather be here than in detention. Besides, what horrible thing is it that I've done exactly? I don't even *deserve* to be punished. I'm just asking the questions that no one else will ask. If the teachers can't deal with it, that's *their* problem.

The trees give way to the open grassland on top of the Samson Cliffs. In the distance, I can see the sheer drop plunging down the rocks into the sea. On the path along the cliff side, Yorrick is stretching and warming up. He doesn't see me yet. I'm still among the trees and his face his halfway turned away from me, the wind whipping around him and his rusty-brown curls dancing in the breeze.

That's when I see a black shape moving at the edge of my vision. A tall figure in a black robe is racing down the costal path coming from the other side. A man wearing a dark mask. A man looking just like the Unbelievers as described to us by the priests – dark and sinister.

My mouth goes dry. I can't believe my eyes. Someone from across the Wall? What is he *doing* here?

Suddenly, it dawns on me the figure in the black cloak is heading straight for Yorrick, who clearly hasn't seen the man yet. I start running toward him. "Yorrick! Watch out!"

I'm screaming my lungs out, but the headwind is scattering my words and they don't reach my cousin. He clearly doesn't hear me, because he's bending down to stretch his calf muscles.

Before I can shout out again, the masked man rams Yorrick in the side. My cousin loses his balance and staggers sideways, teetering on the precipice.

And then he disappears over the edge.

My entire body freezes as if petrified, my eyes not quite registering what just happened. That Unbeliever attacked Yorrick for no reason. He threw him off the cliffs.

And if I don't kick into action and hide right this instant, I might be next.

On shaky legs I stumble backward, but there's no need. Yorricks murderer turns around and runs down the costal path in the opposite direction. He hasn't noticed me.

As soon as he's gone, I take a few tottering steps toward the sheer drop. Tears are pooling in my eyes when I stumble to the edge of the Samson Cliffs and fall down on my knees. The sea is roaring and swirling below me, but that's not where Yorrick ended up. I can see his body, smashed against the rocks rising up from the break. Thankfully, his face is turned away from me. His whole body looks broken.

I can only hope he died instantly. If he's still alive without me being able to do anything for him, I'd rather not know.

A moan rises in my throat. "Why?" I cry out in despair, banging my fists on the rocky soil in front of my knees. "Damned Mary-Agnes!"

My curse helplessly drifts away on the wind. Panting and sobbing, I crawl away from the cliffs and stagger back to the woods. I have to get to Hope Harbor. I have to find Uncle Nathan, the Bookkeeper.

I am now his successor.

8.

I'M SITTING on the docks, waiting for the boat to return – the longboat my dad hastily prepared to salvage Yorrick's body. My uncle and my father left five minutes ago. They asked me if I wanted to join them, but I couldn't. I'm sick with tension and my hands are gripping the edge of the quay so tightly my knuckles have turned white. I stare blindly at the horizon. A good thing it is low tide – once the Bookkeeper and my father get to the rocks at Samson, they'll be able to moor the boat at the beach and walk to the cliffs to get Yorrick away from there and carry him back.

When I stumbled into Uncle Nathan's residence a half hour ago, I couldn't utter a single word besides 'Yorrick is dead'. Once my dad appeared at the scene, I incoherently told them it had happened at the Samson Cliffs, right at the spot Yorrick always went to go running.

I haven't told anyone about the Unbeliever I saw, because I'm afraid I'd cause a war to break out if I did. My uncle is devastated. In his state of mind, he would most likely raise an army, tear down the Wall and burn down everything beyond it. But it won't do us any good at this point. It won't bring Yorrick back.

"Greetings, my son," a voice behind me says.

I turn around and see the three priests coming up to me with solemn faces. The oldest of the three brothers, Praed, puts a hand on my shoulder in consolation and grips it for a second.

"Our condolences on your loss," his brother Finn adds.

I scramble to my feet and shake hands with each of them. "Thank you," I murmur.

"What a tragic accident," Praed says gently. "I wish we'd had the chance to bless him before this happened. Yorrick didn't visit the temple for a long time."

I nod absent-mindedly. What would have been the point? Blessing or not, he's dead.

"Could I ask you something?" Praed inquires.

I give a non-committal shrug.

"How did you find him?"

I am about to open my mouth and tell him about the Unbeliever I saw – the assassin who took my cousin away from us – but then I reconsider. Can Praed keep a secret? Or will he tell Uncle Nathan that our enemies are to blame immediately?

A secret. I close my mouth again, frowning. Why did Praed just say that Yorrick hadn't been round for a long time? He'd been there this very morning. The high priests were supposed to have blessed him the minute he set foot in the temple. Is it a secret he went to talk to them?

All of a sudden the world slows down around me. I see the eyes of the three priests fixed on me – too intent to look genuinely pitiful. They want to know how I found Yorrick. They want to know what I may have seen. And they are purposely concealing Yorrick's meeting with them.

"I agreed to meet Yorrick at the cliffs," I say hoarsely. "But when I didn't see him anywhere on the path, I started to worry. And then... then I saw part of the cliff's edge had crumbled off. I..."

Praed puts his hand on my shoulder once more. "I'm deeply sorry for you, Walt. I know you were close friends."

I heave a doleful sigh and wipe at my eyes. "We weren't that close anymore. He wasn't like himself. This morning he didn't even show up for school. I don't know what was going on in his head." A tear rolls down my cheek. I have never been so grateful for my acting talents.

Praed nods sympathetically. "Boys at that age... They don't talk to anyone. Don't take it personal."

I nod mutely.

"We'll see you at his final journey," Bram pipes up, the middle brother."Take care."

I shake hands with them again before they turn around and leave the quay. I narrow my eyes and stare at them warily as they walk away. My suspicion has been aroused and its seed lies slumbering at the bottom of my heart. What a coincidence that the Unbelieving killer looked *exactly* like the bogeyman of myth and children's tales about the other side of the Wall – a shadow from the dark recesses of our minds, shaped according to the priests' description – because no Unbeliever has ever been sighted for real.

Yorrick confronts the priests with his revolutionary plan and not a day later he is thrown off a cliff. Call me crazy, but I don't think that is a twist of fate. Under no circumstance should I let it slip that I knew of Yorrick's plans, because I am his successor and they are watching me.

I have to keep quiet and be as inconspicuous as possible.

***

That evening, all of Hope Harbor has come out to be present at Yorrick's final journey. My uncle and aunt are standing next to the funeral vessel in which Yorrick's body is laid out, their eyes red-rimmed from sorrow. Yellow flowers adorn the white sheet drawn over his corpse. His body is so wrecked that my uncle thought it best to spare the Hope Harborers from that dreadful sight.

"Sail away now, my son," Uncle Nathan speaks, his voice grave and muffled at once. "Seek out the current of eternity and find your way to Annabelle, she who will welcome you with open arms."

Aunt Agetha is crying softly into a frumpled handkerchief. Yorrick is their only child. She is inconsolable.

Praed comes forward to push off the funeral vessel. Yorrick's final resting place is taken away by the strong current in Bryher's Bay. Before long, the sloop containing my cousin's dead body has disappeared on the horizon. A week from now the smaller dinghy bearing gifts from our family will follow, to make sure he'll be well-off in the afterlife as well.

Yorrick is on his way to the Island of Souls. Or maybe he will wash up on the shores of Cornwall, that mysterious land he longed to see. The World across the Waters is waiting for him. I burst out in tears when Grandpa Thomas takes my hand and whispers: "Faith, hope and love to Yorrick."

When I close my eyes, I can still see his handsome, broad smile. The stories he told me about his father's books are still with me, his enthusiastic voice telling me about his plans still ringing in my ears. And right at that moment, standing there in Bryher's Bay, I decide to honor those memories in the best way possible.

Even though I've lost faith in the Other Side myself, I will see Yorrick's plans through. I'll tell my father about them in secret, and he will help me build a three-master without informing the temple. Perhaps I'll even include Uncle Nathan in our plans once I know for sure I can trust him not to blab to the priests. Alongside that, I will have to prepare for my future task of Bookkeeper and become my uncle's assistant so I won't raise the priests' suspicion.

I will watch them closely. And sooner or later, I will cause their downfall.

Part 2 – Spring Tide

9.

"WALT!"

I distractedly glance up from the book I'm reading. Besides me, Uncle Nathan, and a few administrators, nobody is allowed into the library. I don't recognize the voice, so I wonder who it is.

The man entering the room is weather-beaten and suntanned – a docker, heading toward me with urgency in his step.

"Your father has sent for you," he pants when he gets to the reading table. "It's your grandfather."

I slam the book shut. "What? What's going on?"

The man shrugs. "He's asked for you."

That's all I need to know. Grandpa has been ailing for over a month. The doctor said he's done all he can – some diseases come and never go in old age.

Outside, the heat immediately covers me like a blanket. Since the library walls consist of large, rock-like stones, it's always cool inside, even in the heart of summer. The transition is brutal. I haven't even reached the end of the street yet when sweat is pooling in my armpits and dripping down my forehead, but I don't care. I run even faster. I have to get there in time.

Night after night, I kept watch over Grandpa Thomas until my father finally sent me away, saying I needed a break. It feels like a cruel twist of fate that he's taken a turn for the worse in the first weekend I've managed to get to the library and focus on the Bookkeeper's books again.

When I turn into my street, Dad is waiting for me outside, his face a pale mask.

"Go upstairs quickly," he says before I can ask him anything. "He's hanging by a thread. The doctor is with him."

Grandpa Thomas's bedroom smells musty with fever. Doctor Carl has lit a cone of incense to clear the air – the same incense they always burn at the temple. That will surely comfort my grandfather.

On the bed is a man who was once strong and powerful. Now he looks as if he has already passed away. His face is sunken, his eyes glisten feverishly and his lips are dry and chapped.

"My boy," he whispers when I take his hand, all brittle bones. "You're here."

"I'm here, Grandpa."

He exhales deeply. For a very long time he remains silent, but then his lips part and his eyes open. He stares at me intently. "Walt, promise me you will look for Annabelle. When you sail away."

I feel tears well up in my eyes. A few days ago, I finally confessed to Grandpa what's been keeping me so busy in the past two years. How Dad has been helping me and confided our plans to a few of his friends so they could help design the three-master.

"I'm not sure Annabelle really exists, Grandpa," I say honestly. Maybe someone else in my position would have lied, but I don't want my final words to him to be insincere.

Grandpa smiles feebly. "Then look for something else that will fill your heart with joy," he croaks. "You are an adult now. You are older and wiser than before, but you have also grown bitter. And trust me, you are much too young for that."

I stifle a sob and nod solemnly. "I will, Grandpa Thomas."

My gaze drifts to the window looking out over the harbor. Of course our three-master is not at the docks – we've hidden the ship in a bay on the north coast called St Martin in the old books. No one ever ventures out there because the ruins at the top of the rocks next to the beach are supposedly haunted. We're not superstitious about the place, but most people are, so they stay away. It was the ideal spot to work on our ship. I wonder when we'll be able to sail away on her at last. So many hours of work have gone into designing and creating the *Explorer* – mainly put in by people who have regular day-to-day jobs and are only able to work on the ship in secret by night.

Although it wasn't strictly necessary, I've created a figurehead for the ship. For weeks I've worked on my woodcarving of Yorrick's likeness – he would have wanted to be on board this ship with all his heart. Like this, he'll be with us in a way.

When I glance at my grandfather again, he is no longer breathing. His eyes are staring up at the ceiling, but they don't see anything. No sadness, no pain, no fear. He looks peaceful. Thanks to his faith, he wasn't afraid of death.

I get up on unsteady legs and fumble toward the landing to fetch the doctor. "It's over," I simply say.

Doctor Carl bows his head. He enters the room to close Grandpa's eyes and wash his body before he will make his final journey to the Island of Souls – the place where all those who have passed away wait until the Goddess and her daughters come to save us.

I'm only eighteen, but I feel so much older now that an entire generation above me is gone. Grandma passed away last year. Alisa and I attended her final journey ceremony; Grandpa was a no-show.

"You should tell your father it's over," the doctor calls out from the room. "He went into the garden."

My feet slowly take me downstairs. When Dad sees my face, I don't have to say anything. He gets up from the garden bench and hugs me tightly. "We'll miss him," he says in a gravelly voice. "I would have liked to tell him all about what we'll find on the Other Side."

Sometimes, I have terrible nightmares. I dream we're sailing on the *Explorer* together, my dad and I. The further we get, the clearer it becomes that we won't ever see another coastline. And just as we decide to turn around and go back to Tresco, our ship dips over the edge of the world, plummeting down into a maelstrom of deep and cold darkness.

Of course I hope we'll find something on the Other Side, but I still don't really believe we will. In the meantime, I've seen that map Yorrick told me about back then. I only carry the title of Bookkeeper's assistant, but once my uncle decides to retire, I will take over his job. The fact that I am eighteen doesn't mean I will automatically succeed him next year. I'm not a direct descendant.

I asked Uncle Nathan about the nature of the map detailing the sea around our island and the coast of Cornwall. He told me that the Bookkeeper who ruled Hope Harbor eighty years ago had been a very religious man. He assumed that particular book was a test of our faith – were we to put our trust in some map from the old books or in the promise made by Annabelle? He also related to me that a ship had left for the legendary land on the map and had vanished without a trace. Reason enough for the Bookkeeper in those days to proclaim that we should never think we know better than the Goddess.

Needless to say, I haven't disclosed my plans to sail out again to Uncle Nathan. I also haven't told him I know more about Yorrick's death. He probably wouldn't believe me anyway if I informed him about my suspicions.

"I'll notify the funeral home," I say in a subdued voice. "Tomorrow night, Grandpa will make his final journey."

That afternoon, the bells toll when the Timekeeper sounds them in honor of Grandpa. It is his task to make known to the citizens of Hope Harbor who has passed away. The people working for the funeral home will collect Grandpa Thomas and prepare the funeral vessel for tomorrow's ceremony.

It doesn't take long for Alisa to ring my doorbell. She knew how bad Grandpa was doing, so it's not hard to guess for whom the bell tolls. Her arms envelop me in a gentle embrace and she smiles at me sadly. "You only have one parent left," she says, a quiver in her voice. "I'm so very sorry for you, Walt."

"I'm all right," I reply dolefully. "It's okay. He was ready to go."

Together, we go upstairs to my room. I was never that close with Samuel, but Alisa and I have become best friends since Yorrick's death. I never told her what I saw that day on the cliffs, either, and it eats away at me. Very often, Yorrick's murder also still features in my dreams. The edge of the world and the edge of the cliff that killed Yorrick; those two recurring elements populate my nightmares in all kinds of shapes and sizes. It feels as if I am also teetering on a precipice, waiting for someone to push me off or for myself to gather enough courage to make the jump.

Today, I am taking the leap. It's about time.

"I have to tell you something," I admit to my best friend. "Promise me you won't tell it to anyone else."

Alisa's eyes widen. "Okay."

In the hot summer afternoon, I grope around for words to begin. A fly keeps buzzing up against the glass in the window, hoping to fight his way outside. It wants out, but it doesn't know it is trapped.

Am I doing any better because I *do* know?

"Yorrick had great plans," I start. "He found this map in the Bookkeeper's Library – a map detailing land northeast of Tresco."

Alisa gapes at me. "You mean the Island of Souls?" she whispers deferentially.

I shake my head. "It's not an island. Not as far as he could see, anyway. It's called Cornwall, and Yorrick wanted to build a big ship and sail there. If Annabelle doesn't come to us, we will come to her, he reasoned."

Alisa has taken a seat on my bed, her eyes fixed on the wall where I have a portrait of Yorrick in a frame. "He was so restless," she mumbles. "I didn't understand what it was he wanted. I thought maybe I could be what he was looking for. I hoped I could make him happy."

"And you did," I assure her. "He was very happy with you. But he also wanted to find out the truth, give it to the people and broaden our horizon. That's why he arranged a meeting with the high priests one morning, so he could tell them about all the things he wanted to change once he turned nineteen and became Bookkeeper. And that very same day, he was murdered."

Alisa's head jerks up. "*What*?"

"I was meeting him at the Samson Cliffs," I rush on nervously. The look in her eyes frightens me. "He was just doing a warming-up when suddenly, out of nowhere, this masked guy in a black hooded cloak showed up. He tossed him over the edge. He pushed him."

She jumps up, her face a twisted mask of anger. "He was attacked by an Unbeliever? And you didn't *say* anything?" she snarls. "Are you out of your fricking mind?"

I trip backward. "Listen to me," I say urgently. "I don't think it was an Unbeliever at all. Something didn't feel right."

"What do you mean?"

"I thought it was way too convenient for Praed and his brothers that Yorrick was pushed off a cliff by a masked man in black only a few hours after his confrontational talk with them." When her eyes widen even more than before, I push on. "Come on, Alisa – have we ever actually *seen* an Unbeliever? And why would one of them only come out to kill a boy who had no significance to them whatsoever?"

The fury is still evident in her blue eyes. Suddenly, she steps forward, her fists pummeling my chest. And then, she breaks down and starts to cry. "You should have said something," she sobs helplessly. "Why didn't you *say* something?"

My legs tremble when I lower myself onto the bed. "Because I was scared out of my mind. And still am. If Praed, Finn and Bram ever catch the slightest wind of what I suspect, they'll make sure I disappear too. None of them knows that Yorrick told me his plan, and I'd like to keep it that way. Besides, I'm executing his plan in secret."

Alisa swishes her blonde hair out of her face and sits down next to me, her cheeks still tear-stained. "You're building a ship?"

"Yes, I am."

"A ship nobody knows about?"

"Well, of course some people do. My dad and a few of his friends. The Bookkeeper doesn't even know."

She shakes her head disbelievingly. "Yorrick was killed and you didn't even tell his father? Walt, that's horrible. He has a right to know. And he should most definitely know about the Priests' reign of terror."

"But I don't have a single shred of evidence to support my allegations," I respond dejectedly. "It's just guesswork. I'll never know for sure whether they did kill him."

"We'll see about that." Alisa gets up and takes my hand. "We are going on an investigation. I want you to take me to the crime scene. Show me where everything happened."

Alisa wants to study to become a Peacekeeper next year. She has a strong sense of justice, but she also has a keen nose for clues. If anyone is able to help me with this, it's her.

"Fine." I let her pull me up and follow her out the door. "But we can't be seen by anyone, understand?"

10.

OF COURSE, the first part of the path takes us past the temple. When we get to the fork in the road, we turn left. The air feels hot and stifling and it's taking my breath away. The skyline is obscured by dark clouds.

All the way up to the grassland above Samson, I keep looking over my shoulder to make sure we aren't being followed by someone working for the temple. It might be a bit paranoid, but I've tried my very best to behave inconspicuously in the past two years. The idea that one of the priests might find out I'm a witness to their murder is making me edgy, to say the least. I'm afraid my face will show that Alisa and I are not just casually walking here. I've stayed away from these cliffs ever since Yorrick died.

"This is where it happened," I say, pointing at the coastal path stretching out ahead when we come out of the woods. "I was still between the trees when that man in disguise ran up to Yorrick from the other side."

Alisa walks to the edge, peering at the hill to her left sloping down away from us. "And he was coming straight at Yorrick?"

I nod. "He fled along the coastal path toward the east, down those hills."

"In the direction of the Wall," Alisa says, her mouth set in a grim line. We know the coastal path doesn't continue all the way to the Wall – at some point, it veers off to the right, leading down to a tiny bay wedged in between two steep cliffs – but Alisa is right: it does come very close to Unbeliever Territory.

Without commenting any further, Alisa starts down the coastal path. And for at least an hour, she keeps walking – further than I have ever gone down this trail, further than anyone has ever walked. Why would they? We all know the path comes to an end at a barren and desolate bay. However, that doesn't seem to stop her. With pent-up anger in her stride, she rushes on as though the masked murderer is still waiting for her at the end of this road, two years after his attack on her boyfriend.

In the distance I can hear the thunder rumbling. The first drops of rain are starting to fall on the path in front of us. "Shall we go back?" I shout against the wind. "We'll be caught in a storm."

She ignores me. Annoyed, I start walking faster to catch up with her. "Alisa! Just stop for a minute, will you? What's the point of doing this?"

"I want to know," she pants. "I want to know what happened. I don't want to return as long as I don't know, Walt." She starts to cry.

I fall silent and take her hand. And then we continue together. The thunderstorm has now fully erupted, rain lashing down on our heads. We end up on a small beach between the rocks, both soaked to the bone. The sea crashes onto the sand in foaming, angry waves.

"Now what?" I ask despondently.

Alisa squints against the spray, peering to the left. She takes a step forward and pulls me with her. "You know what? I think there's a hidden cave in the cliffs over there. You see how the waves break differently at that spot? There's got to be some sort of cavity or opening in the rocks. Maybe we can find shelter there."

I smile for a moment. A nose for clues – that's what I thought before. With our backs pressed against the rocks of the cliff, we carefully edge toward the cave we will hopefully find. The salty water splashing up stings my face, but at least it doesn't claw at my feet. The ledge we're on is high enough, and to my amazement, it really seems to lead straight into a cave partially hidden from view by the plants growing on the rockface, drooping down from the overhang. From the beach, it's nearly impossible to make out the entrance.

Inside, the cave is cold and murky, but at least it is also dry. The sound of water breaking against the rocks echoes off the walls of the cave. I follow Alisa, who cautiously shuffles forward until the ledge grows wider so we can walk next to each other.

"What is *that*?" she suddenly exclaims.

The ridge runs into a smooth floor worn out by seawater. Ahead of us is a plateau, but that's not what caught Alisa by surprise. Several wooden crates are stacked on the natural platform. It's obvious we are not the first people to discover this cave.

My heart speeds up when I approach the chests. Fortunately, they don't seem to be locked. What's stashed inside those crates? Could they belong to Unbelievers?

And then Alisa grabs my arm. "Walt," she whispers in shock. Her hand trembles when she points at one corner of the cave. I follow her gaze and my breath hitches.

Rows and rows of dinghies are piled into the corner. No longboats or sloops for passengers, but the small boats we use in temple services to send gifts or offerings to Annabelle and the deceased. The dinghy on top of one of the piles still has its decoration of white and yellow flowers on either side, partially wilted and eaten away by the seawater. The lowest dinghy in the pile has rotted away almost completely.

I shiver, but it's not because of the cold. "How the heck did they end up here?"

We both gape at the pile of dinghies in utter bewilderment.

"The current," Alisa mumbles with a vacant face. "The current takes them here."

Ever since I can remember, Praed and his brothers have taken us to Long Ledge, a wild patch of beach and grassland where beautiful flowers grow all year, even in wintertime. That is the place where we always assemble to send off the dinghies with gifts for our deceased family members on the Island of Souls, because tradition associates the Beach of Flowers at Long Ledge with the Goddess. It is a magical and awe-inspiring experience to watch the small votive vessels bob away on the waves – except it now turns out we've always mistakenly assumed they'd float away to a place beyond our reach.

"Those *thieves*," Alisa sneers in barely contained anger. "All the precious fabrics are gone. All the boats are empty."

I was expecting all kinds of things, but strangely enough this comes as a bolt from the blue. "You think... this is the *priests'* doing?"

Alisa laughs scornfully. "Yeah, who else do you think? Some Unbelieving savages who crossed the Wall and stumbled on these boats and all the valuable stuff by accident? Mary and Agnes on a raft, this is *disgusting*."

She rubs her face tiredly. I'm lost for words. The priests are stealing from Hope Harborers in mourning. They're secretly using fabrics that were meant for our dead relatives. Textiles that people worked hard and saved up for, so they could clothe the dearly departed.

"Want to bet they have that red piece of cloth lying around here somewhere? The gift I sent Yorrick one month ago to let him know I haven't forgotten about him?" Furiously, Alisa wipes away her tears and stalks over to the nearest chest. She yanks the lid open but freezes on the spot.

"What? What is it?" I whisper anxiously when her face goes pale.

Slowly, Alisa pulls some fabric out of the crate. In one hand she is holding a finely-woven woolen blanket in yellow, but her other hand is clutched around a black cloak.

The mask that was tucked away in the folds clatters to the floor and stares up at me with hollow eyes.

11.

I DON'T know how long exactly it takes for us to sort out the textile in all the chests, but when we're done I feel as if years have passed. We've made a separate pile of fabrics we recognize from sacrificial temple services of a few weeks back. Woolen cloth that Praed and his deceitful brothers haven't had the time to pick apart yet.

We discovered balls of yarn in one of the larger chests. They used to be garments. Obviously the priests couldn't parade around in jackets and pants that the townspeople might recognize.

Wool is the most expensive good in Hope Harbor. There aren't enough sheep to supply the entire population with woolen clothing, and some people put in extra hours for months on end just to be able to send a deceased parent one single woolen blanket, while making do with rough garments of sackcloth themselves. The sight of all these piles and piles of stolen wares makes me sick.

"You think we have enough proof to convince your uncle?" Alisa asks with a dark look in her eyes. She puts the black disguise on top of the pile. Goddess only knows how long *that* deception has been in effect – is it possible that the former priests taught Praed, Finn and Bram how to dress up as Unbelievers so they could scare people into piety and submission? Or did they come up with that brilliant idea all by themselves?

"You bet," I mumble. "As soon as we get home, we'll show our find to as many people as possible. Everyone should know."

Since we're planning on exposing the priests' fraud anyway, we don't go to the trouble of erasing our tracks. All the crates are still wide open when we leave the cave. We carry the smallest one together – that's the chest we used to put all the evidence in.

Outside, the ledge is now slick and slippery due to all the seaweed coughed up by the sea. "Be careful," I call over my shoulder. My one hand grips the handle of the chest I'm carrying behind my back; I use the other to find support against the rockface.

Very slowly, we shuffle back down the length of the ridge while carrying the heavy chest. By the time we make it to the beach with our spoils, my knees almost buckle from exertion and anxiety.

Alisa puts the chest down on the sand with a groan. We're lucky the rain has stopped. It was a quick but heavy summer storm – big clumps of seaweed are lapping back and forth on the waves foaming at our feet. As I look closer, I suddenly see it's not just seaweed. There's wreckage. Lots of it. It's bobbing around in the surf, and when I look at the horizon, I see more bits and pieces of a ship floating to the surface.

"Holy Agnes," I blurt out, my heart slamming against my ribcage. "One of our ships was lost, Alisa! Have a look at all the driftwood."

My best friend peers at the skyline and pales. "Damn, you're right. Who could have sailed out that far? The welcome committee is supposed to sail out in two days' time, right?"

"Yeah. That's strange."

I see movement in the distance. A bird? A large fish? Intently, I peer at the black stain on the blue-gray background of the water. It's an arm. Arms. Someone is swimming out there!

"Look, it's a survivor," I yell in a panicked voice. "A castaway. He's still alive."

Without hesitation I kick off my shoes and pants and dive into the water. I may not have sealegs, but I am an excellent swimmer. I wrestle with the waves in order to get to the drowning man as fast as I can, but I can't see him anymore. Where am I supposed to go?

"To the right!" Alisa hollers from the shoreline right at that moment. I adjust my course and quickly swim on. The survivor of the shipwreck is clinging to a bright-blue object that looks like a big chest but is somehow floating on the water.

"Hey!" I call out to him. "Hold on. I'm here to help you."

When I've reached the odd-looking container, I prop one shoulder underneath the man's armpit to steady him. He looks up at me, and I blink my eyes in utter astonishment.

I have never seen this man before in my life.

"Come on," I try to encourage him when I snap out of my paralysis. "Swim as fast as you can."

We start to kick out at the water while using the strange, blue object as a life buoy. The man is panting and gasping with effort. He doesn't seem to have a lot of strength left in his legs, but he's obviously doing the best he can. His deeply tanned hands – how many days has this man spent in the sun to end up looking like that? – are gripping the blue chest tightly. His hair is black as night. His eyes are as brown as his skin. This is not a Hope Harborer. Could it be an Unbeliever? Does this mean they have ships, too?

After what seems like an eternity, we finally find ourselves on the beach. Coughing and shivering, I drag the man toward the safe sand. Alisa takes a blanket from our crate and uses it to dry us both. Afterwards, she puts a warm coat on the man. If she's puzzled by his appearance, she is doing a good job of hiding it.

When the man finally speaks, his first words are: "Where is Henry?"

"Was there someone with you on your ship?" I ask uncertainly. I hope I understood him correctly. He has a very strange accent.

He nods wordlessly. "That storm. The waves were so high. We drifted past the island... and then our ship caught on an underwater rock."

There are indeed rocks under the water a little ways away from the island. Our sailors avoid that particular spot, mostly because it is too far to the east. Too close to Unbeliever Territory. Could it be true – did the other people on the island try to build a ship of their own so they could sail away?

"Where are you and Henry from?" Alisa inquires curiously.

The man turns his head to look at her. "My name is Tony," he says hoarsely. "And I'm from the mainland."

"The mainland?" I echo nonplussed. Main as opposed to what?

Tony just nods. "From Cornwall."

That's when the bottom drops out of my stomach and my heart speeds up with excitement and joy all at once. I can't believe my ears. So it's not a lie after all – it's real. Yorrick was right. There really *is* something beyond this island. And this man came from that legendary land.

"Can you walk?" I ask.

"I guess, but not very fast," he says with a feeble smile.

"No problem," Alisa chimes in, her voice shaky. "Walt and I need some time anyway to discuss what we're going to tell our people." She looks past Tony and shoots me a perplexed look.

A chest full of incriminating material and a man who really knows what's true of the stories about the World across the Waters – this could turn out to be a very, *very* black day for Praed and his companions.

12.

ALL THE way back to Hope Harbor, I can feel a warm hope growing in my heart. Even though Alisa and I discovered our spiritual leaders are charlatans, we also found out our way of life isn't completely based on an untruth after all. There is an Other Side, and there are people living there who have come to look for us. At least, that's what I think – and with that thought, a part of my faith in the culture of Hope Harbor has been restored. We're not that crazy after all.

Alisa is carrying Tony's chest, which turns out to be very light. When I asked him what the thing was made of, Tony said: "Plastic." It looks like the old objects in our museum, the things that used to belong to our ancestors and were utilized in day-to-day life when they built a life here for themselves.

I'm carrying the crate stuffed with woolen fabrics. Tony is too weak to help us; in fact, he's leaning heavily on me as we make the steep climb from the beach toward the top of the cliffs.

"Where could Henry be?" he asks, out of breath. "Are there more beaches along the south coast, or is it just rocks and cliffs?"

I shake my head. "There are beaches, but we never go there."

"Oh." Tony frowns. He leaves it at that, and frankly, I'm happy about it. I'll need my time to explain it all to him. First of all, I want to focus on getting home in one piece and warning my dad and uncle.

When we get into Hope Harbor, the streets are quiet. The thunderstorm has chased everybody inside. That's fortunate, because it means we don't have to deal with inquisitive eyes seeing Tony just yet. I only realize my dad isn't even home yet when we turn into our street. He's having a wake for Grandpa in the room where they keep his body before the funeral home closes its doors tonight.

"If only Grandpa Thomas had lived one more day," I mumble to Alisa when we step inside. "He would have been able to see people from the Other Side with his own eyes."

Alisa puts down the blue chest and smiles up at me. "Your grandpa will see the Other Side with new eyes and in a new light now, Walt. Don't worry."

I nod and smile ruefully back. Then I point Tony toward the bathroom and put on a kettle to fill a tub so he can freshen up. I lay out fresh, dry clothes for him and advise him to get a good rest. He has hardly spoken a word, and I know he'll have to say a lot more once other people will show up here wanting to bombard him with questions.

"You go get my dad," I instruct Alisa once we're outside again. "And I'll notify the Bookkeeper."

***

I find my uncle sitting in the library. When he looks up at me, I see a hint of tears in his eyes. The book full of maps of the land and the sea is on the table in front of him.

"I'm sorry," I stammer nervously. He must be thinking of Yorrick. Uncle Nathan often gets lost somewhere deep inside himself when we read from this book. "I don't want to bother you, but I have to. I have important news."

He closes the book and cocks his head curiously. "What's the matter, Walt? I already heard about your grandfather, you know."

"It's not that." I sit down and stare hard at my hands. "Uncle Nathan, I know more about Yorrick's death than I've let on."

A deep silence pervades the room. When I finally risk glancing up, my uncle is staring at me, his face white as a seagull. Why doesn't he say something?

Surely he doesn't think *I* have something to do with his son's death?

"I saw someone pushing him," I quickly go on. "A man disguised in a black cloak and a mask.

Yorrick was killed, after he'd arranged a meeting that same morning. He was meeting up with the high priests to talk about the maps you were just looking at. And I found that disguise today. In a cave that is used by Praed, Finn and Bram. I'm sure they are the culprits."

Uncle Nathan stares at me with hollow eyes. And then he softly starts to sob. I look at him in bewilderment and get up to walk over to him. I had expected rage, not sadness. "What's wrong, Uncle?"

"I knew about the meeting," he cries. "Yorrick told me just before he left – about his plan to sail to the Other Side once he was the new ruler. When he fell off the cliffs, that afternoon, I feared there was a connection, Walt. I was so confused. But I couldn't imagine it was really true. I didn't *want* to imagine it. I should have stopped Yorrick from going. I should have interrogated Praed afterwards." He slams his fist down on the tabletop. "I shouldn't have let my feelings of guilt drag me down. I should have *done* something."

I put a hand on his shoulder. "There's more."

As I tell him of the quest Alisa and I went on, the cave we found and the chests containing expensive clothes as well as the Unbeliever disguise, the color slowly returns to his cheeks. He is livid – his eyes are bright with anger.

"So they are murderers *and* scoundrels," he says grimly. "This has got to stop. I am going to drum up some Peacekeepers so they can go to the temple and take those three frauds into custody right now. All these years… they've been lying to me all these years."

When he gets up, I follow him. "You should probably send a messenger, Uncle Nathan."

He spins around. "What? Why?"

I inhale and cringe a bit. "There's *even* more."

He slumps back into his chair. "Well, bring it on."

"We found a castaway. He was fighting for his life in the sea near the cave. He's the survivor of a shipwreck; his ship was lost in the thunderstorm."

"Not one of us?"

I shake my head. "Someone from Cornwall," I reply, a tremor in my voice. "And he lost his shipmate, a man named Henry, who most likely washed up on Unbeliever shores."

"A man from the Other Side?" Uncle Nathan's eyes are bulging so much I'm afraid they'll pop out of his sockets. "Has he mentioned Annabelle?"

"He hasn't mentioned much of anything. He almost died. He's recovering back at our place, and I think we should go talk to him – you, me and Dad."

My uncle opens the book again and flips the pages until he gets to the map of Cornwall. "They have come," he says, stroking the paper reverently. "They have finally come. Dear Mary, Agnes and Martin, holy Annabelle." Suddenly, he freezes and his head snaps up. "But their ship was lost in the storm."

I nod slowly.

"So they can't take us back," the Bookkeeper continues, his voice strangled. "They are trapped on this island, just like us."

I draw a deep breath. "No, they're not and we're not. Because I have a ship too – a vessel big and robust enough to take us all the way to Cornwall."

13.

WE ARE gathered in the living room. Alisa busied herself preparing dinner after getting back home with my father. There's a big dish with fish, potatoes and carrots on the table. Tony is starving and polishes off two plates before we subject him to a round of questions. Actually, we don't have to ask him much – he's rested now, and eager to tell us his story.

"Henry and I are from Bodmin in Cornwall," Tony starts. "That's a settlement rebuilt by survivors about one-hundred and forty years ago."

"Survivors?" Alisa parrots hesitantly.

"Yes... survivors of the epidemic and the bombs." Tony looks around the circle of faces and visibly pales. He must recognize our complete puzzlement. None of us have a clue what he is talking about.

He frowns and rubs his forehead. "Tell me – what's in your earliest recorded history?"

"This island was made for us," my uncle immediately drones, sounding like one of the priests. "Annabelle brought us here and she will come to take us away again once we're ready. Many generations have come and gone, but the Goddess hasn't yet appeared. We've been waiting for one-hundred and fifty years."

Tony nods. "Okay," he mumbles.

"I take it you've heard of her in Cornwall as well?"

Slowly, the man from the World across the Waters shakes his head. "I'm afraid not. Your Goddess is unknown to us."

In the ensuing silence, Tony gets up and walks over to the kitchen to get some more yoghurt and blueberries. We are all so visibly thrown by the news that he must have decided to leave us alone to process it by ourselves. I raise my eyebrows at my dad. He feebly smiles back.

"So our stories aren't true?" Alisa whispers defeatedly. "Does this mean the priests have lied about *everything*?"

"We don't know that," the Bookkeeper objects. "The fact that this man doesn't know Annabelle doesn't mean she doesn't exist at all." He doesn't sound too convinced, though.

Tony returns with his dessert bowl and slowly sits down again. "Why don't I tell you about history *before* Annabelle?"

"That seems like a good idea," my uncle nods bravely. "I'm all ears."

"All right then." Tony clears his throat. "Hundreds of years ago, the world was a very crowded place. There were billions of people, and they were continuously waging war on each other. At some point it got so bad they wanted to annihilate each other with fire and disease."

Tony spins us a grim story of how people used to live. Leaders didn't just fight each other, but dragged their subjects into wars that would never yield one real winner because the weapons they used were deadly to all and everything. Famine, poverty and injustice reigned supreme.

Slowly but surely, his story is making me sick with sadness and disappointment. Is *this* where we came from?

"So you're saying our ancestors were criminals," I suddenly blurt out, interrupting his story. I can't listen to it anymore.

Tony shakes his head. "Not at all," he quietly replies. "Your ancestors were pure and innocent. They were children."

My father blinks dazedly. "All of them?"

"Yes, all of them." He reaches for the blue chest, which Uncle Nathan has put next to Tony's chair. He opens the lid and takes out a pile of paper. It looks old... even older than our books.

"Henry is an apt technician," Tony explains. "He fixed an old radio in Bodmin – the kind of thing they used before the war – and one day, he picked up an old signal, a transmission that was recorded one hundred and fifty years ago." Apparently, he once again notices our looks of incomprehension, because he goes on to wave away his own words. "Never mind. It's kind of complicated. A radio can pick up spoken words across great distances, let's put it that way. The signal we received was an SOS message on auto-repeat originating from Penzance. So we went there to find out more about the broadcast."

He pulls the book with maps toward him and points at a dot on the map. It's on the coastline and marked with a red circle. I never wondered about that red circle before, but now I do.

"What we found was a deserted harbor without any ships or boats. There was also a main building with an improvised graveyard next to it." Tony's voice turns more solemn. "The adults had all come down with a sickness that had somehow not infected the children. That's why a ship full of healthy kids was sent to this island to outrun the disease. They were supplied with all the basics – livestock, seeds, books about ship building, agriculture, animal husbandry and hunting skills. The adults waited and waited for the ship to return so the healthy people among them could rejoin the children. But the ship never came. And the kids' parents all eventually died."

"What's in those papers?" Uncle Nathan wants to know.

Tony spreads out the sheets on the table. There are three large ones. "This is the ship's manifest. It lists all the cargo on board, as well as the captain in charge, the passenger list and the name of the ship, obviously."

My eyes absorb the words written in the manifest. It is in an ancient handwriting and hardly legible, but I can still decipher the language. Everybody is getting up to pore over the documents. I notice the name of the captain – Nathan Wortley – and can't help but smile for a moment. Apparently, it is a name fit for authority figures. And now I'm wondering whatever happened to the old Nathan. He must have sailed away to get the rest of the people, because there are no remains of an old boat anywhere in our harbor. He might have been sick before he sailed out; that's why he never made it back to Penzance.

There are more familiar names on the passenger's list – William Yorrick, Thomas Samuel, Sara Praed. We were named after our ancestors, a ship full of kids trying to flee the epidemic.

At that instant, Alisa inhales sharply next to me and grabs my arm. "Walt, look," she says, a strange quiver in her voice. "Look at the name of the ship."

My eyes dart to the first line on the manifest. And immediately, I understand the shock that's evident in her voice.

There she is.

Annabelle. Our Goddess.

***

By the time we are done talking, the sun has set and our world has changed beyond recognition. Whatever caused our recorded history to diverge and become so radically different from what really happened will most likely never be fully understood, but I don't think that's the most important thing. For me, the most sensational news is that the Other Side really exists and that we can actually get there.

"I want to have a serious talk with the priests," the Bookkeeper says. "And once I'm done with them, I want the entire population assembled in the village square. They need to be addressed." I nod and follow him in my capacity of Bookkeeper's assistant.

When we get to Hope Harbor's central square, however, it turns out assembling the townspeople is no longer necessary. All the people have gathered on the square, huddled together in front of the gates to the Peacekeeper's detention center. The news about the priests' scam has spread like wildfire. Everybody is outraged, demanding justice.

"Please, citizens of Hope Harbor, may I ask for your attention and beg you to calm down?" Uncle Nathan calls out over the clamor of the shouting crowd. He has brought the horn we always use to begin important announcements with. The deep, trumpeting sound rolls over the citizens amassed on the square. Slowly, the noise peters out to a dissatisfied grumble.

The Bookkeeper and I get onto the little stage set up for trials next to the prison. I have no idea what he's going to tell the Hope Harborers, and judging from the look he shoots in my direction, he's not too sure about it himself.

"My dear citizens of Hope Harbor," he starts nevertheless, "today, many things happened and much was revealed. I would like to start with the most important thing. My nephew Walt saved a man from drowning this afternoon. A man who came from the World across the Waters."

As he's talking, the three high priests are being ushered on stage by a score of Peacekeepers. If my uncle still wants to address the priests, he can do so right away.

"Is he one of Annabelle's Heralds?" a man in front of the stage calls out. "Has he come to call Praed into account?"

Some other people shout their agreement. Threatening fists are raised in anger, now that the people can see Praed, Bram and Finn lined up behind us.

"No, he isn't," the Bookkeeper replies, his voice ringing out clear. "This man, who goes by the name of Tony, has ventured out from Cornwall with a friend of his. Cornwall lies north-east of Tresco. He came here in a small ship, but it was lost in the storm. He narrowly escaped drowning. And he doesn't know Annabelle."

His last few words linger in the air, spelling a painful truth. The looks cast at the priests are even dirtier now. I turn around and my gaze lands on Praed's ashen face. His eyes are full of tears and his lips are trembling.

Before anyone can stop him, he steps forward and jabs at the Bookkeeper's arm. "She… she doesn't exist?" he stammers, his voice barely above a whisper.

"The *Annabelle* was the ship that brought our ancestors here, one-hundred and fifty years ago," my uncle replies softly. "I haven't been able to find out more than that, but I do know she's not a Goddess and she certainly doesn't live in the World across the Waters."

Praed closes his eyes, his jaw tightening.

"You miserable thief!" the baker suddenly bellows from the front row. He lost his wife not six months ago. "You dishonest, horrible sneak! I've been breaking my *back* earning the money for that dress I sent out to Eliza! You said she'd get it in the hereafter. You said Annabelle would take care of her, but she doesn't even live on the Other Side! You and your brothers… you've been robbing us blind, stealing and picking apart my dead wife's dress."

Praed looks straight into the baker's eyes and takes another step forward, bringing him dangerously close to the edge of the stage. He's standing there as though there's an abyss beyond it that he simultaneously craves and fears.

And then, time seems to speed up. Someone from the crowd grabs his ankles, and Praed falls down on the floorboard. Someone else seizes him by the waist. Before the Peacekeepers can intervene, Praed is being dragged offstage, disappearing underneath a horde of people taking out their anger on him.

I let out a cry and rush forward to try and pull the infuriated people off him, but in vain. "Please! Stop it!" Nobody seems to hear my plea for mercy.

I turn when I feel a hand on my shoulder. With tears in my eyes, I look up at Uncle Nathan.

"Let him be, Walt," he mumbles. That's when it dawns on me what it is we're watching. Praed *wanted* this. He moved so close to the edge because he knew what would happen.

Strange but true: it looks like he always believed in the Goddess despite his appalling actions. And Tony has now taken that away from him.

Feeling sick to my stomach, I turn around. I can't watch this self-flagellation any longer. "Please put the other two back in their cells," I snap at the guards who are carefully shielding Bram and Finn from the multitude. My legs tremble when I walk down the steps and head for Tony. He's standing next to Alisa, watching the violent spectacle with his mouth agape.

"Let's go and find Henry," I say.

"Don't you need to stay here?" Tony asks.

I shake my head. "I don't think so. The Bookkeeper will have to solve this. He's supposed to take care of the people as long as he's in office. And besides, someone should think of you, too. I'm going to help you, and what I'm about to do is about as dangerous as what you're witnessing here. I'm going to enter Unbeliever Territory."

"Unbeliever?" Tony parrots dazedly.

"I'll tell you the story on our way home."

Nobody notices us as we leave the square.

14.

BY THE time we get back home, I've decided to go by myself. Tony still isn't feeling well after his near-drowning, and quite frankly, I *want* to do this alone. Ever since that one time I went back to the Wall at age fifteen, I've felt like I had to cross it one day.

"Take this with you," Tony says, handing me some sort of round, silvery bar.

I shoot a hesitant look at the thing. "What am I supposed to do with this?"

He moves my thumb so it touches a switch on the side and pushes it upward. Suddenly, a beam of bright light emerges from the bar. It's as clear as daylight.

"It's a flashlight," Tony explains. "You should only use it if it's really necessary – I have no idea how long the batteries will last."

"Excuse me?"

"How long the light will keep shining."

"Ah. Okay. I'll use it sparingly."

I push the switch down again and slip the flashlight into my coat pocket. Then, I shake Tony's hand firmly.

"Henry is quite tall and he has red hair," Tony tells me once more. "When you show him that flashlight and tell him you were sent by me, he'll join you in a heartbeat."

If I find him, of course. I'm not convinced I will. If I could comb the entire coastline without encountering any trouble, I might stand a chance, but I can't be seen. Admittedly, I don't really believe in monsters dwelling in darkness on the other side of the island anymore, but I don't think the Unbelievers will welcome me with open arms either.

I walk as fast as I can. Once I'm under the trees, I slow down because I can hardly see a thing. Every now and then, I use the flashlight to help me find my way. The small, miraculous circle of light is dancing on the path ahead and makes me wonder about the world Tony came from.

It's good to know we haven't waited in vain for all those years. We haven't been forgotten. I still don't understand much of the radio message our ancestors left behind all those years ago – Tony even brought a device that could play the message for us, so we listened to it earlier this evening – but one thing is certain: there were once people who cared about us, and there still are today. Otherwise, Tony and Henry wouldn't have come. They wanted to show us the big, wide world.

What's also occupying my thoughts is the question whether the Unbelievers are related to us.

Were they already on Tresco when we arrived, or was there some kind of conflict in our history that caused a number of our ancestors to move to a different part of the island?

After a tough trek through the dark woods, I end up in front of the Wall. Slowly, I shuffle to the right, looking for the footholds in the Wall I used to pull myself up before.

It takes a while for me to find them, but I do. I gulp down a big lump in my throat before putting my foot in the lowest hole. This is it. I'm going to cross over.

Very carefully and quietly, I climb up and lower myself on the other side. I don't hear anything except a hooting owl and the rustling of leaves in the wind. My heart is beating fast as I enter the forest I saw the sheep disappear into. That animal belonged to someone, so there must be people living here. I hope they're friendly. For all I know they've been very helpful to Henry and no harm has come to him.

When I stumble on, my ears suddenly pick up a strange, wailing sound. It's coming from behind some bushes. Could it be an animal?

I quickly hide in the undergrowth and try to make out shapes in the dark, but that's hopeless. I do realize that the sound isn't coming from an animal, though – it's a human voice crying out in agony. A young boy or a girl, by the sound of it. My palms are slick with sweat when I grab Tony's flashlight and decide that the best defense is a good offense. Wounded or not, this person is from the other side of the island, and we've been warned about them.

I spring up from the bushes and turn on the flashlight at the same time. The pale face of a girl is caught in the dazzle of the lightbeam coming from the device. She looks familiar to me, but I don't exactly know why. Her eyes are wide with fear, and I can see she's about to scream. I take another step forward and clamp my hand down on her mouth. "Be silent," I snap at her.

Suddenly, it hits me why she looks so familiar. With her bright, blue eyes and jet-black hair, she looks exactly like Annabelle. Could this be a sign? Does it mean I can trust her?

"If you promise not to scream, I'll let go of you, okay?" I hiss at her.

She nods slowly.

As soon as I take my hand off her mouth, she pushes the lamp away. "Could you please take that... that *thing* out of my face? You're blinding me!" She mumbles something about some guy named Luke that I don't quite understand. She has a strange accent, just like Tony. "What *is* that thing? And who are *you*?" she continues.

"My name is Walt. I got this lamp from one of the shipwrecked men." She gives me a dazed look. "The man who washed up on our side of the beach. Across the Wall?"

I'm still not getting much of a response. I lower the flashlight and shine it on the nearest tree. "And who are you?"

"I'm Leia. I live in the manor house."

"You live on this side of the Wall?" I ask, just to be sure, and she nods. I let out my breath. "My Goddess, you're an Unbeliever. So you guys *are* real, after all."

She takes a step back and shoots me a dirty look. "Yeah, and apparently, so are your people. You're one of the Fools."

I can't help it – I start laughing. Her indignant face combined with the name they've given us... it makes the tension drain out of my body. "None taken," I tease her lightly. "Is that what you call us?"

The girl with the Goddess face stares hard at the ground, shuffling her feet uncomfortably. She looks scared and stressed. What could be the matter with her? I'd ask, but of course, I didn't come all the way here to question *her*. I have to know what happened to Tony's friend.

"Listen up," I say in a serious voice. "I'm actually here looking for someone. A man in his forties with reddish hair. Is he with your people at the manor house?"

She glances back up, her eyes filled with suspicion. "Why?" When something rustles in the bushes next to us, she suddenly grabs my arm in a panic. "You have to put out that lamp. They're looking for me. They shouldn't find me."

All right then – I'm obviously not the only one in trouble here. Leia audibly sighs with relief when I turn off the light.

Why is she running? It's as if she's scared of her own people.

"I did see that man," she says softly, "but that's not the reason I'm on the run." Her eyes well up with tears.

On impulse, I take her hand and try to comfort her. "So why are you? What happened to you?"

She tells me about a book she has stolen from her leader – a book she secretly wanted to read and then pinched when she was almost caught in the act.

I can't help but chuckle. "So what were you planning on doing with it here? You can't really read it in the dark, can you?"

She gives me a withering look. "You know, for a Fool you're pretty smart."

I scoff. "The only reason you're calling us foolish is because you've never been on the other side of the Wall. You don't know anything at all."

"Oh, right. And you do? We're not Unbelievers at all. That's such nonsense."

We both pause for breath. This is the strangest conversation I've had in a long time. That Leia girl is pretty prickly, but I guess she's like that because she's scared out of her wits.

"I wouldn't mind finding out more about you and where you came from," she finally admits quietly. "But I have to hide the book first." She emphasizes the word as if they only have one tome in that entire manor house of theirs.

"Why don't you give it to me?" I suggest on a whim. Actually, I'm sort of curious to find out what the thing looks like.

"To *you*? Why should I?"

"Like I said, your people never cross over. So I bet that leader of yours won't think to look on the other Side of the Wall."

"But… I haven't found the writings I was looking for yet," she replies timidly.

"Well, how about this? We'll meet up tomorrow at this very same spot. I'll bring your book and you promise to bring a smile."

That shuts her up for a moment. Maybe she didn't realize how snappy she's being with me. Leia hands over her book. "So what do you want to know about this Henry?" she says more pleasantly.

I tell her about the shipwreck and about Tony and Henry landing on each of our shores. As I'm telling her my story, she grows even more quiet and pensive. It's clear something is bothering her, but I don't know what. Again, I take her hand in mine to reassure her. It's been a while since I held a girl's hand, apart from Alisa's. Somehow I feel the urge to protect Leia. She reminds me of a frightened and stressed baby bird, despite her crabby comments and bravado.

And then she says something that startles me. "Henry is being kept prisoner in the manor house. I think he may have told our leader some stuff that Saul didn't like very much."

They've *imprisoned* poor Henry instead of helping him? What's *wrong* with these people? I shake my head in disbelief.

"Let's meet here around noon tomorrow," Leia proposes.

"Fine with me. I'm going to report back to my people in Hope Harbor. That's where I live. With a little luck, a couple of strong men may volunteer to come with me to rescue Henry from that manor house you live in."

Leia gives a curt nod. "The Force be in you."

I cock an eyebrow. What a strange expression – although it sounds kind of beautiful. "Faith, hope and love," I reply. I shake her hand one more time and then I swivel around to head back to the Wall.

I am completely and utterly confused. It was easy to pretend in front of Leia – I acted like I knew what I was doing or what was to be done, but I don't have a clue. The man I set out to look for isn't untraceable – he's out of reach. Some crazy guy is holding him captive in a manor house. But *why*?

I try to imagine what would have happened if the situation were reversed. If Praed, Finn and Bram had found the castaway, would *they* have taken him back to Hope Harbor and let him spout his story about a Cornwall without Annabelle? I seriously doubt it. In all probability, they would have kept him in that cave for the rest of his life so he wouldn't have had a chance to test our faith. Praed might even have decided to silence Tony forever for taking the Goddess away from him.

I shiver when I think back to the moment Praed was dragged off the stage. I don't pity him – after all, he murdered my very own cousin, or had him murdered at the very least – but the despair and the dejection on his face instilled me with such sadness.

For the first time since I've saved him, I'm wondering whether the appearance of Tony in our lives is such a blessing after all.

15.

I DON'T get much sleep that night. All the hours of darkness are filled with agitated voices of people in the streets. My uncle and father take turns in calming down the Hope Harborers, trying to address questions that no one can answer yet.

Early in the morning, I get up and put on my mourning clothes to attend my grandpa's final journey. A few days ago, I prepared a little box for Grandpa Thomas with scrolls of holy scripture inside. I'd intended to send that to him in a few weeks' time, but instead I'm taking it with me now. Putting it in the funeral barge is the only way it's guaranteed to be with him, wherever he goes in death.

My father is waiting for me downstairs. His eyes are puffy due to lack of sleep.

"Please leave most of the work in town to Uncle Nathan today," I advise him as soon as I set eyes on him. "You should get some sleep."

He nods shortly.

Once we've left the house and are on our way to Bryher's Bay, Alisa and her parents join us on the path leading down to the sea. My best friend looks washed-out.

"Have you heard what happened to Praed?" she whispers.

I nod solemnly. He didn't survive his fall into the crowd. The Peacekeepers don't know who specifically gave him the death-blow, so there won't be any criminal prosecution – his death was deemed an accident. It doesn't sit well with me. Even though Praed was seeking out what happened, it still feels to me like we're getting away with murder unpunished.

"Who's going to lead the final journey ceremony?" Alisa continues.

"I have no idea."

"Well, is there any point left in doing the ceremony? The whole story is a lie, anyway."

"Alisa, stop it," I burst out to her. "Of *course* there is a point. If *anybody* in this town deserves a final journey with all the frills, it's my grandpa."

She looks up at me, her eyes startled and contrite. "I'm… sorry, Walt. You're right. I just don't know what to believe in anymore. What to value."

I give her a pensive stare, and in a flash, Leia's words come back to me. "We should attach value to ourselves," I softly say. "Because there's a force within us. In me, in you. In the world around us. We can put our trust in that."

A tear rolls down her cheek. "If you say so."

I put my arm around her shoulders. "I say so."

***

Grandpa's funeral vessel sails when the sun comes up in all its glory. The Bookkeeper gives a touching speech about the horizon not seeming that far away anymore. He claims that all the deceased who have taken the journey before us will always be with us, and live on within our hearts.

When I step forward to speak, some people are already shedding some tears in anticipation. Everyone knows how strong the bond was between me and my grandfather. But before I speak of my grandpa's life, I want to say something else. Something that turns out to be important to me, and it surprises me as I speak the words.

"I want to ask you urgently not to cause any havoc in or around the temple," I say in a steady voice. "Thomas went there every week. No matter how deceitful the priests may have been, I think the place we all went to in order to pray and celebrate solstices has to remain intact. It has been a sanctuary for many. Now it's time to give it new meaning."

After that, I talk about Grandpa and the things he did for our community. My words seem to calm the people down, and I'm thankful I've at least managed to do *something* about the angry and violent mood in our town.

I look sideways at the barge that contains my grandfather's body. When his ship sails, my world will never be the same. His old stories will disappear, but one of them will stay and is now more relevant than ever: the story of Toja. Once upon a time, she crossed the Wall, and it's about time we do so too. Even if it's only to spring Henry from prison.

The question my history teacher once asked us in class comes back to me – the question that triggered me to snap at him and leave school early so I witnessed Yorrick's murder. He wanted to know whether Annabelle should take pity on the Unbelievers and visit them too, or if she should turn her back on them because they didn't deserve a second chance.

Leia's frightened face is etched in my memory.

I think they still deserve another chance.

***

Tony is waiting for me in the living room when I return home at ten o'clock. He puts a hand on my shoulder when I sit down. "My condolences on losing your grandfather. I didn't know where you were. One of the neighbors told me."

I nod briefly. "I'm sorry I haven't been able to tell you what I discovered last night yet. It was late when I finally got home."

I get Leia's book from the cupboard next to the fireplace. Judging from the picture on the front cover, the story is about people with magical powers. They're holding weapons made of light. Maybe these are their gods?

"This island is divided into two areas," I start tentatively. "I told you that last night."

Tony nods. He claimed that the Wall dividing Tresco had already been here before our ancestors came. One half of the island belonged to a wealthy man who'd fenced off his manor and grounds from the western part of the island, and particularly from the village and harbor that people used to visit with their 'pleasure yachts' in summer. Apparently, people used to sail for fun in the olden days. I can't really imagine why.

With a grave face I show him Leia's book. "Yesterday, I ran into an Unbelieving girl who had run off into the forest with this book. She said her name was Leia, and that the book was important to their leader. She wasn't supposed to have it."

Tony takes the book from my hand and his eyes widen. With a baffled face, he stares at the front cover, his lips twitching like he's trying to hold back a smile. "The people on the other side of the Wall have to be descendants of the first settlers as well," he says. "Nobody lived here anymore when the *Annabelle* set sail for Tresco. You all belong together."

"That's what you say, but they don't see it that way. They call us fools. And the people running the manor are dangerous – Leia told me they're keeping Henry prisoner. I have no idea if they're open to negotiations."

Tony frowns, scratching his chin. "How big of a chance is there of getting Hope Harborers to help us storming that manor house?"

"Not too big," I mutter. "First of all, people are still scared of what's behind the Wall, and secondly, we have enough trouble on our hands here as it is."

Tony sighs. "That's what I thought. Let's see how things play out for the moment. But tell me, why did you bring that Star Wars notebook here, Walt?"

When I stare at Tony vacantly, he nods at Leia's book. "I mean that book, of course. I have to tell you, I know the people on the front cover pretty well."

A small stab of jealousy goes through me. The Unbelievers, of all people, have a book filled with heroes that *are* known in Cornwall? "Are they people from Bodmin?"

Tony laughs out loud. "No, they aren't. Well... it's a long story. I guess I'd better explain it to Leia..." He suddenly pauses, looking at the book again. "... first," he finishes, still sporting that partly-amused, partly-baffled smile.

"I can invite her to come here. And I'll also ask her to keep an eye on Henry for us," I say.

"You're going to meet up with her now?"

"Yes. We agreed to meet at noon."

"Well, in that case I wish you good luck. I hope she has news about Henry, or even better, that she can make it to Hope Harbor, hopefully together with him."

16.

I'M TOO early. When I get to the spot where we've agreed to meet, I don't see anyone. Fortunately, I'm dressed for a stake-out in the woods – all my clothes are green. This used to be my father's hunting outfit when he was a bit younger.

I eat the honeycake I brought with me. Just as I'm about to take a bite of my pear, I hear voices, so I put the second half of my lunch back in my bag. Why *am* I hearing voices? Isn't Leia supposed to come alone?

From my hiding place in the shrubs I keep an eye on the trail between the trees. It doesn't take long before I can make out two girls carrying baskets full of wild plants and leaves. On the left is a blonde girl who is curiously looking around, and on the right is Leia. I blink in astonishment. Wow – in broad daylight, she looks absolutely beautiful. Her black hair gleams in the sunlight and her blue eyes are clear as the summer sky.

"Leia," I call out quietly, stepping out of the bushes and raising a tentative hand. She sees me shooting a glance at her blonde friend.

"She's my best friend," Leia quickly explains. "She also knows you have the book."

The girl giggles for a second and introduces herself as Mara. I shake hands with her and then turn back to Leia. Goddess, I can't keep my eyes off her. She's probably wondering why I'm gaping at her like an idiot. Yup – she's turning red. Now I really feel like a dork. When Yorrick was still alive I often felt like this next to him, and those days still aren't behind me, it turns out.

"Did you bring it?" she wants to know.

I show her my winning smile and hope I haven't turned red myself. "Of course. And I've got some news for you: Tony knows your ancestors."

"He does?" Leia's mouth falls open, her whole face looking so radiant I suddenly don't feel envious anymore about them having a book containing something true. She looks like she could use a boost.

"Yes, and he wants to talk to you about it. Explain things. You think you can gather a few friends you trust and come to us in Hope Harbor?"

As soon as I mention the name of my native town, her face clouds over. Do they really hate our people that much?

"I guess we don't have a choice," she replies, sounding none too happy.

"Oh, I'd *love* to!" Mara pipes up next to her, who doesn't seem to hold the same grudge against us. Oh well – at least I managed to impress *one* girl.

Leia elbows Mara in the side. "But we should address our own problems first. Force our leader out, free Henry, consult with the parents…"

I blink my eyes in surprise. What a strange way to mention her mom and dad – like she doesn't feel close to them at all. "*The* parents?" I repeat dumbly.

"Yeah. They live in Newexter." Leia stares at her feet and continues in a softer tone of voice: "You know, I wouldn't mind if they decided to step in and help us."

Now I can really feel my jaw drop. "So you don't live with your parents?"

"No. Of course not," she snaps back, as though I asked her a completely silly question.

"But how old are you girls then?" I insist.

"Fifteen and sixteen."

Every Unbeliever for himself. That's how the saying goes. They don't need any help… not even the children? "I didn't know it was that bad," I stammer, confused.

"Bad?" Leia glares at me as if she wants to bite my head off.

Oh, man. This conversation is *not* going the way I'd hoped. I can't help feeling the need to defend myself. "Yeah, don't *you* think it's bad?" I retort.

Her face falls. I think I hurt her feelings, and I regret it instantly. Why can't I just be *nice* for a change?

"So you *do* live with the parents?" she inquires uncertainly.

I nod. "Yes, we do." I put my hand on her shoulder for a moment and she rewards me with a tiny smile.

The girls sit down to read in the book, and I kind of feel like the fifth wheel. From what Leia said to Mara, I've concluded Henry is still a prisoner. I should probably report this back to Tony and the Bookkeeper, but I also want to know more about the girls' conflict with their leader and what is written in that book of theirs.

I'm leaning over Leia's shoulder as she discusses the content of a few pages with Mara. It feels *good* to be near her. In a different way than when I hang out with Alisa. She and I are just buddies. With Leia, I feel a sort of tension in the air that thrills and unnerves me at the same time.

In the meantime, Mara and Leia are all riled up, heatedly arguing about a certain passage in the book that seems to be very important to them. "Luke's father tried to accrue all power for himself. He became a bad and dark leader. However, collaboration makes us the strongest, so no leader is needed to work together," Leia reads out loud, her voice shaky. Hey, it's that Luke again.

"That's it," her friend exclaims. "That's the proof we were looking for."

I clear my throat. "I guess we're not that different after all," I observe cautiously. It feels good to be able to say that – who would have thought? "Although we don't know any Luke. The Bookkeeper is our leader, and he's a direct descendant of the first Bookkeeper on the island."

Mara looks at me in wonder. "Wow! Your people have a book, too?"

I nod, shooting Leia a Yorrick-smile. "More than one, actually. They're a bit like this book, but the words look neater. Very precise." So precise, in fact, that no one has ever been able to copy the exact script from the books in letters and pamphlets. The first Bookkeeper must have been a skilled man with a very steady hand. "Full of knowledge about the World across the Waters."

Leia swallows. "Is there anything in those books about us?"

No, there isn't. I've wondered about that peculiar fact ever since I started studying the Bookkeeper's library – the only books that seem to mention the Unbelievers belong to the priests and are in the temple, allegedly. Their stories have unfailingly been accepted as truth. "It is said that the Unbelievers turned away from us because they don't believe in the World across the Waters. Or rather, they don't think anyone from that world will come for us. You want to determine your own fate and be on your own."

She gives me a pensive look. "So we once were together? The Fools and the Unbelievers?"

"Once upon a time." And all of a sudden, I wish we could be together again. It's nonsense we have been afraid of what was on the other side of this Wall for so many years. We've been blinded by fearmongering. The very few people who did risk crossing the Wall – like Toja – have never come back, but maybe they should have. Our world would have looked very different today.

"What should we do now?" Leia asks her friend. "Shall we tear out that page?"

Mara starts. "No, we can't damage the book!"

"Seems like a bad idea if you want to use it as some proof in a trial," I say, winking at her playfully. "How else would your people know it's from your book?"

Leia shoots me a withering look and the smile freezes on my face. "Of course we'll keep the book intact," she snarls.

"Let's hope no one will do a body search," Mara whispers.

I frown, suddenly worried. "Okay, sounds like a plan. But please will you be careful?" My eyes search Leia's face, and she looks surprised by my concern. She bites her lip and nods slowly.

"Will you come to Hope Harbor soon?"

She nods again. "When will you have time for us?"

I shoot her another – hopefully charming – smile. "For you? Always. I'm the Bookkeeper's nephew, you know, so everyone knows me. Just ask for Walt."

"I will," she mumbles.

I take a step toward her. "And Leia? Try bringing a smile next time, okay?" I tease her.

I'm half-expecting another snappy remark, but it doesn't come. Instead, Leia slowly turns red. She nervously takes a step backward and grabs Mara's arm. "Come on, let's go," she says. At once, she whips around and picks up her basket before trotting off.

A bit dazed, I stay where I am, staring at her retreating figure. A proud smile threatens to split my face in two.

I made her blush. Maybe she doesn't think I'm such a dork after all.

My feeling of accomplishment is quickly followed by annoyance at my own trivial thoughts, and I kick a tree stump in exasperation. Why am I even thinking about that? My biggest priority should be to reunite the Unbelievers and the Hope Harborers. And if that noble task will enable me to get to know Leia a bit better, that's an added bonus.

A fairly big one.

17.

WHEN I return, the town is still in as much chaos as when I left. People are running around everywhere, carrying boxes and crates.

"What's going on?" I inquire when I spot my father talking to the neighbor in front of our house. I walk up to him. "Is this some mass migration?"

"Some people are packing for the crossing," he replies.

"Crossing?" I echo. "What..."

"We told them about the *Explorer*, Nathan and I," my father continues his explanation. "People have a right to know there's a ship waiting for them, now that we know for sure there is an Other Side to get to."

"Oh." It makes sense, and yet it upsets me to see how many people are eager to run away from this place. This is our home, after all. Our world.

"Nathan took some men to the temple," Dad says. "They're looking for stolen goods that might still be hidden in there."

Clothes that were meant for the dead – outfits once worn by our religious leaders.

"I think it's nonsense," I say from the bottom of my heart. "Why can't they use their energy for something more useful?"

He sighs. "They're trying to process it, Walt."

"Process what?"

"Everything. This." My father gestures at the wide-open front doors around us, the people rushing out of their houses, carrying bags and chests filled to the brim with their possessions. Cracked statuettes of the Goddess are lying around on the street, face-down in the dirt, destroyed in a fit of rage.

"Well, I suggest they make an effort to process things differently," I reply angrily. "It seems we're forgetting there is another part of this island, filled with people who might want to know the truth as well. And Tony's friend still hasn't returned – in fact, he's a prisoner. Don't we need to help him? Without Henry, we never even would have met people from the Other Side. He picked up that message, didn't he?"

My dad smiles warmly at me. "Well, I suggest you call up a meeting. You've been the Bookkeeper's assistant for quite a while now... maybe it's time you put more weight behind decision-making around here."

"I will. Thanks."

I elbow my way through the baggage-carrying throng of people crowding the street. On my way up to the temple, I'm grateful for the sea breeze cooling my hot face. Annabelle's Breath – I can still hear Grandpa calling it that.

On the road leading up to our sanctuary are more shattered figurines.

And suddenly, the urge to see my grandfather one more time hits me like a wave. I miss him so terribly. And I miss the Goddess just as much. I know it sounds stupid, but I miss believing in something, even though I more or less lost my faith years ago. There's a gaping hole in my heart because no one will ever again enter the temple and find solace by gazing up at the murals that have been there since the dawn of our history. Is there really no higher power taking care of us, or is that power a force from deep within us?

Or is there nothing at all?

My last words to Grandpa were a promise. I said I'd search for whatever brings joy to my heart. And whether that is a force from within or from without, I can't do it all by myself.

Leia's book put it very clearly: collaboration makes us the strongest.

Once I'm inside the temple, I am happy to discover the place is not just riddled with angry people plowing their way through piles of clothing. In the corner of the great hall, next to the bookcase containing all the scripture, Alisa is perusing some books in her lap.

"Hey, you!" I sit down next to her and give her a quick hug. "What are you doing here? Defending the holy books?"

She shrugs with a shy smile. "Something like that. I think it's important to safeguard these books. I still think there's wisdom in them. And they're a part of our history. I just wanted to make sure nobody would set fire to them in a fit of rage. Not after your speech at your grandpa's ceremony."

I smile at her, deeply touched. "You're amazing," I say softly.

She chuckles and waves away my words. "Suck-up. Your tricks don't work on me, you know."

"Tricks?" I bat my eyelids innocently and shoot her a playful grin.

"Yeah, those tricks you copied from Yorrick," she says with a suddenly serious face. "Sometimes, you behave just like he did because you want to impress people."

"Oh, come on," I protest. "They worked on *you*, didn't they? You loved Yorrick."

She shakes her head and pauses for a moment. "I fell in love with him because I could see right through his mask."

Alisa clamps her lips together. She doesn't want to talk about Yorrick anymore, I think. Instead, she reaches for an ancient-looking book that's lying on the bench beside her. She opens it on the very first page and shows me a drawing. "I found something."

My eyes take in the picture. It's a primitive illustration of the Goddess. She's standing on the prow of her boat, her arms spread out like a bird's wings. The sides of the ship in this picture aren't decorated with flowers. Beside the boat, the name *Annabelle* is written in simple letters.

"There's a story written by a girl on the next page," Alisa says, pointing at it. "Someone called Mary. She writes her mom will come back on a boat one day."

Is this a book that once belonged to the first Bookkeeper? The child that took care of the chest full of books that the captain left us? Once again, my eyes scan the drawing. And for the first time, I can see what our temple murals represent. I understand why this drawing was made, so very long ago.

"This is how our legend started," I whisper. "The name Annabelle didn't belong to the woman in this drawing, but to the ship. Mary was one of the stranded kids, not a saint."

Together, we stare at that very first picture made on the island, drawn by a hopeful child waiting for her mother. A tear silently rolls down my cheek.

I close the book.

"I have a plan," I say. "We're going to visit the Unbelievers and tell them everything we know. Hopefully we'll set Henry free in the process." I point at my uncle. "And the Bookkeeper will help us accomplish that."

18.

IT HAS grown dark outside by the time we are all gathered in the main meeting room – the Bookkeeper, some Peacekeepers, Alisa, my father and the few muscly dockers who helped us build the *Explorer*. Tony and I are seated at the head of the table.

"My nephew has called us together to organize a rescue mission," Uncle Nathan starts his story. "He has been to the other side of the Wall, has spoken to a few easterners and has learned that Henry, Tony's shipmate, is being held captive by a dictatorial leader for unknown reasons."

We've decided to start using a new name for our neighbors. Most Hope Harborers themselves have turned into 'Unbelievers' by now.

The head of the Peacekeeping committee turns his head to look at me. "You've been there? What was it like?"

"Strange," I reply with a half-smile. "The first person I bumped into looked exactly like Annabelle. Isn't it funny that she had to be the first Unbeliever I should run into?"

"So you met a woman?"

"She's still a girl. And this morning, I spoke with her again. Apparently, the children in their community live separately from the grown-ups and they have an oppressive leader. It's all very bizarre, not to mention alarming. The leader in question has taken Henry captive."

The Peacekeepers all start talking at once until my uncle calls them to order. "If we want to launch a rescue mission, we'd better do it straight away," he says. "The darkness will give us enough cover to try and get to that manor house without being detected, so we can break in."

"Agreed, but how are we going to find it?" my father objects.

Uncle Nathan turns toward me. "Have you asked that girl to meet you here?"

"Her name is Leia. And yes, she said she'd try to come here with a few friends who are brave enough."

"So she could show us the way?"

"She could." I pause for a moment, thinking hard. "But what are we going to do about the easterners? Don't we need to tell them about the two men from Cornwall?"

"What, you suggest we go talk to that eastern leader who went off the deep end?" Jim, one of the dockers, retorts. "For all we know he might lock us up too."

I shake my head. "*He* might be crazy, but his subjects aren't. Come on, Jim, those girls were both

132

terrified. They need our help. They have just as much right to getting off this island if they want."

Some ruckus in the hallway off the meeting room makes me swallow my next few words. The door flies open and on the threshold stands Joseph, the old man who runs the sheep farm. "Walt," he's panting, sweat dripping down his brow. "You have to come with me."

With a thumping heart, I get up. "Why? What's wrong?"

"A girl has crossed the Wall. An Unbeliever. She's asking for you."

"Well, who is she?"

"I don't know her name," he stammers. "She has black hair and she's wearing a brown dress."

That's all I need to know. If Leia decided to show up here at this hour all by herself, something is not right. I turn around to face the Bookkeeper. "Find as many people as you can who want to help us on the other side of Tresco. The more, the better. Let's meet up at the harbor."

Before my uncle can ask me any more questions, I storm out the door. Joseph can't walk that fast, and I have to force myself not to rush him. He takes me to the town border nearby the forest, which is where his house is.

And there, in a street illuminated by a few lanterns swinging in the breeze, Leia sits on the bench next to Joseph's front door, looking like a sad mess. Her hair is straggly and notted from running through the forest; bits of twigs and leaves are stuck in her long, black locks. There are holes in her simple shoes and I see stains of blood on the worn-out leather.

"My Goddess! Leia, what happened to you?" I sit down next to her and pull her against me. She's shivering – from fear or exhaustion, I can't tell – and then she breaks down crying. "Are you alone?" I try again. "Where are your friends?"

Sobbing, she slumps against my shoulder. "He... is... dead," she hiccups.

"Who's dead?"

Her breath falters. "Henry. Saul killed him."

Leia's words knock the wind out of me. This has gone on long enough. We have to do something, and we have to do it right *now*. It may be too late for Henry, but we can still save the others. We must get every single innocent easterner out of there immediately. After all, we're supposed to be one people, and Leia and her friends belong to us. We all belong to each other.

"That does it," I say out loud. She looks up at me with tear-stained eyes. I squeeze her arm encouragingly. "We're going in."

Part 3 – Flood

19.

BY THE time we reach the harbor, I've learned a lot more about Leia's life. She's told me that her brother and friends are still in danger, and I hope with all my heart we'll be able to do something for them. I also told her a bit about life on our side, although it has radically changed in the past few days. She looks around in amazement and seems completely overwhelmed by the whole experience.

She takes offense when I question her people's willingness to believe in whatever she sees on this side of the island. I'm starting to see through her crabby behavior and reactions, though – she thinks I'm looking down on her, judging her way of life for being stupid.

When we board the *Explorer* – which is at anchor in the harbor now, thanks to my uncle – she gapes at Tony with wide eyes. Dark-skinned people like him must be as much of a rarity on her side of the Wall as they are here.

I poke her in the side. "You seem impressed by his appearance," I tease her a bit sourly.

"Yes, he looks so otherworldly, doesn't he? So different and so... handsome," she quietly replies.

"Hmm." I could have done without that last observation.

She glances aside and her eyes search my face. "I thought you looked really striking too when I first met you," she says, a sudden sparkle in her eyes.

"You didn't look at me this mesmerized," I chuckle, but it sounds forced. Great; I sound like a jealous three-year-old – it's definitely cringe-worthy.

Leia crosses her arms and narrows her eyes, shaking her head. "How would you know? It was way too dark to see my face."

I take a step closer and turn on the charm by showing her my most amiable grin. "Oh, so you *were* enthralled by my obvious beauty?" I say more softly, letting my voice drop.

This doesn't have the desired effect. In fact, she shies away from me, the corners of her mouth turning down. "No, I wasn't *enthralled*, Walt, I was scared out of my mind. I still am. I mean, my brother and friends could be *dead* for all I know, and you think this is the time to use some cheap come-on tricks on me?" Her cheeks are flushed red. "I bet you think you're really cool for scoring yet another girl," she concludes, her voice wavering. I can't hear whether she's angry or disappointed.

I shrug sullenly. "Sure. And of course you weren't even a tiny little bit drawn in by it," I mumble, cocking my head and looking at her inquisitively.

Her face flushes deep red as she barks: "I'm going to talk to Tony." She quickly whips around and makes her way to the foredeck.

Well, I'll be damned – Alisa might be right. Throughout my teenage years, I've trained myself to imitate Yorrick's demeanor whenever I felt insecure. That's when I turn into a swaggering big-mouth that's not really me. Maybe Leia can see right through *that*, the way Alisa could see past Yorrick's mask. That's why she is so put off by my attitude – because it's fake. Because it doesn't suit me. Maybe it's time to leave my mask behind. What do I need it for? What am I afraid of?

My eyes scan the harbor I have spent so much time at that I know every jetty and every footbridge. The lighthouses are still alight with fire in the distance, even though we're no longer waiting for anything to show up. It seems at least *some* traditions are still being kept alive.

I only move away from the railing when I spot my uncle walking up the quay, directing a large group of men onto the *Explorer*. Leia is still talking to Tony, so I have to interrupt their conversation for a moment.

"The Bookkeeper found men who are willing to fight," I tell her, pointing at the army of Hope Harborers gathered by the gangway. "Now you need to be our navigator."

Leia told me that the young easterners' parents were probably willing to help. I still can't quite wrap my head around the fact that they don't meddle in their kids' affairs at all – if I understood correctly, children in their culture are supposed to be self-sufficient when they turn ten. That is the most ridiculous thing I've ever heard. The parents live in a village called Newexter and Leia's friend fled to that place to avoid an arranged marriage and tell the adults about the horrible things happening back at the manor. We're planning to sail halfway around Tresco to get to their village unseen and ask them to join our troupe.

Our Hope Harbor soldiers are flooding the ship's deck. I don't see Alisa among them, but that shouldn't surprise me. This is going to be a dangerous mission, after all. I still miss her, though.

Dad heads straight for me once he's on deck. "Is that Leia?" he asks quietly, tilting his head at the prow.

"Yes, that's her."

"Remarkable," he mumbles. "She really looks exactly like Annabelle. Why is she standing there all by herself?"

I turn around to look at her. She has put her hands on the railing and is staring out at the horizon. Although she's even younger than Alisa, somehow it doesn't feel like a juvenile girl is leading this expedition. Leia may look like she needs protection at first sight, but she exudes a kind of natural authority. She's got the same flair for leadership that Yorrick used to have.

"We had an argument," I mumble uncomfortably. "She's angry with me."

My father shakes his head at me. "Huh. I bet a sack of wool she's just hoping you'll join her at the prow. Can't you see she's glancing over her shoulder every now and then?"

"Oh. You think?"

"Pfff. Of course. I know what women want," he replies, making it sound as if he is Hope Harbor's most famous ladies' man.

I laugh nervously and throw up my hands in surrender. "Okay, whatever. I'll go to her. You're probably right."

My mouth turns dry with nerves as I slowly make my way toward Leia. When I casually lean against the railing next to her, she glances aside for a moment, but keeps quiet. Above our heads, the night sky is peppered with stars looking like precious jewels scattered on dark-blue fabric.

Yorrick would have been able to break the ice with a very romantic line, I bet, but he's not here. I am here, and I'm not Yorrick. I will have to do this in my own, awkward, clumsy way.

"I'm sorry," I softly say.

"For what?" she asks not unkindly.

Carefully, I put my hand on her fingers clasping the railing like a vise. She must be scared, being on a ship for the first time.

"I bet you think I'm an arrogant showoff," I go on, my heart tapping against my ribs.

"Yeah, I kind of do," she calmly admits.

I feel a blush rise to my cheeks. "Oh."

"Well, you're behaving like one, aren't you?" she shrugs.

"Yeah... that's true."

"But you're sorry about it?"

In a bout of honesty, I decide to spill it all. "Yes, because I'm not like that at all. I just don't know how to behave when I'm around you. So I start acting all tough."

I give Leia a soul-searching look, and to my amazement, she blushes pink. "Uhm, yeah... you know, I kind of recognize the feeling. That's why I act all snappy around *you*."

I let out a deep sigh. Wow, it feels good to be able to be myself. "Will you please stay close to me when we go ashore?" I ask firmly.

She cocks her eyebrow and gives me a playful smile. "And run the risk of you acting all tough again?"

"I'll try to behave," I solemnly swear.

She grins like a brat. "Okay. We're good then."

I put a tentative arm around her shoulder. She's still smiling at me, so I pull her a bit closer and press

141

a kiss to her forehead. I can hear her sucking in her breath, and then she leans her head against my shoulder.

When I turn my head toward the aft deck, I see my dad is watching us with one of his all-knowing smiles. Okay, it's nice we hugged and made up, but I'll make my next move away from prying eyes. I slowly let go of Leia and head for the ship's wheel, where the captain is barking commands at his steersmen.

After another half hour of sailing in the dark, we're there. The *Explorer* needs to move as close to the beach as possible, and once the anchor has been lowered, we take out the longboats and go ashore. I can only hope this Saul guy hasn't posted any guards on the beach wanting to pierce us with spears as soon as we set foot on the sand, but admittedly there's little chance of that. After all, Unbelievers don't expect anything to come from the Other Side – neither friends nor enemies.

Once we've all safely assembled on the beach, Leia takes the lead and heads for a path hidden between the trees. The trail leads straight to her village. The closer we get to Newexter, the faster she walks. There might be bad news waiting for her in the village, but at least she's not shying away from hearing it as soon as possible.

We break out of the trees and blink against bright lights. The entire village seems to light up the dark with big fires, and the Newexter villagers appear to be in turmoil. People turn around to gape at us when we press forward to get to the central square.

An old man with a gray beard and a simple, brown-reddish cloak immediately comes forward to welcome Leia when we get there. Next to him is a woman who looks so much like Leia that this can only be her mother. The woman pulls her daughter into a tight embrace and starts to cry. The old man who looks like a Keeper taps Leia on the shoulder and points at us. He clearly wants to know who we are.

When I come closer, I can hear him talking about a hostage situation. Apparently, some more people haven been taken captive, and one of them is a good friend of Leia's.

"What's going to happen now?" I hesitantly ask when I join her. I smile warmly at the old man and Leia's mother.

Leia turns around and gazes at me. Slowly, I can see a certain look growing in her eyes – a look that's pushing all fear away, only leaving room for indignation combined with determination. That certain air of authority I sensed before is back. She looks around the circle of people gathered around us.

"We're going to the manor house," she speaks in a clear voice, "and we'll break down all the doors and windows so Saul will come out. He has to release

Andy. And if he doesn't, we'll set the building on fire. We'll smoke him out."

Those last words cause a few women in the circle to pale visibly. Oddly enough, they don't start protesting because Leia is suggesting they burn the manor leader alive – they're objecting because the *house* will be destroyed. I whip around to catch the eye of our Bookkeeper and raise my eyebrows at him. He shakes his head imperceptibly. We don't understand their ways, but it's not our place to comment or interfere, either.

A boy with dark hair and blue eyes just like Leia emerges from the crowd. That must be her twin brother Colin. He defeatedly tells her that Saul stole their book again. I wonder how important it will be for them in the future: Tony said he knew their ancestors, so who knows – it might be of benefit to them if they get it back.

And then the village leader – they call him the Eldest – comes up and addresses the Bookkeeper. He has gathered fifty men around him, all holding torches as well as an obvious grudge against the leader of the manor. I bet their children were all maltreated and abused by Saul. Maybe Leia's father is among them too. And what about Saul's parents – are they hiding in shame? The manor leader can't be that old himself, obviously.

"I believe we're going," my father mumbles next to me when the procession of torchmen begins to move. He nods at Uncle Nathan and Tony, and we fall back to form the rearguard with our army of westerners. Between our group and the fighters from Newexter is a group of children – but actually, they are already grown-ups here.

They want to see their former leader burn at the stake.

20.

IT IS a peculiar march of people winding their way through the trees of the forest. There is no talking or shouting at all. In a flash I think back to the moment our three reviled priests were pushed onstage, and the loud, verbal reaction of the crowd that had gathered to demand justice. These people, however, seem to radiate a different kind of rage: grim, internal, and determined. It is as if they're being fed by an invisible force.

And then, the infamous manor house looms between the trees. The white walls are overgrown with moss and ivy, and the windows are all covered by once-green shutters, paint peeling off the slats. The house looks like it is on its way to become one with the forest surrounding it on every side. On the lawn in front of the house, I can make out sagging tents and small huts. It looks like a desolate and gloomy place.

The people in front of us finally start to talk softly among themselves. We push open the gate and enter the grounds, walking up to the main entrance of the building. Leia is all the way at the front of the crowd, frowning at the door. Her shoulders are tensed up in a half-shrug.

Everybody around her becomes quiet as a mouse, and for a moment, she looks back at me over her shoulder, almost as if to ask for help.

The Eldest comes to her aid and demands loudly that Saul come out of the house.

A silence descends on the lawn, but nothing seems to happen. Before the Eldest can repeat his command, stones, branches and torches are being hurled at the manor door by the outraged easterners. The crowd begins to chant: "Let-him-go! Let-him-go!"

All of a sudden, the door opens to a crack. The Eldest yells out for his people to stop their assault.

When a pale, skinny guy with black hair steps outside, my very first thought upon seeing him is: this is a boy who wants to be a man, but isn't quite there yet. The sword he's holding is too heavy for his arm. The hard lines around his mouth don't match the skittish look in his eyes. The cramped hand he's using to hold the rope tied around his captive's wrists betrays his insecurity. Here stands a guy who is broken, and I wonder what caused his ruin.

"If you so much as lay one finger on me, I'll kill Andy!" he cries out in despair.

Leia steps forward. "What is it you're fighting for, Saul?" she asks, the harshness all but gone from her voice. Maybe she has sensed it too – how vulnerable Saul is now that he's standing all alone.

"I'm fighting for *our* world," he barks at her. "A world without help from the Other Side. A world without parents. A world without real love. And *that* is the truth. Don't even try to deny it."

His words are so cold and so lonely that my breath hitches for a moment. When I compared Saul to Praed, I was wrong. Praed lost his faith and threw himself to the wolves, but this boy lost his faith many years ago – and he continued living. He turned into a wolf himself.

"The parents are here for us," Leia swears to him.

Saul laughs scornfully, but then he stops and blinks his eyes to fight back sudden tears. "Yours, maybe. I don't even *have* parents. I'm all alone." His voice cracks.

So that's why no one in Newexter objected when Leia suggested torching the place with Saul still in it.

From the corner of my eye, I see movement. It's Tony. He's fighting his way to the front and glances sideways at me when he passes. With a shock, I see there are tears in *his* eyes, too.

"No, you're not," he calls out, calmly addressing Saul. "You're not alone. Nobody here is. And you may not have a father of your own, but your forefathers loved you and didn't want you to be forgotten."

Saul frowns. "What are you talking about? How would *you* know?"

"I know more than you do."

"Oh, here we go again – another so-called 'visitor from across the sea' who wants to take me for a ride. You *do* know what we've done to your friend for lying to us, right?"

Tony slowly nods. "Yes, I do. And I also know that you're just scared of the world. You can't fight that kind of fear with swords. You can't eradicate it by killing people or bullying them into submission, no matter how hard you try."

In the ensuing silence, Saul gapes at Tony, his jaw slack. For some reason, in this moment Tony reminds me of the most popular teacher in our school: Mr Ferry. He never got angry with pupils who behaved badly. He always wanted to make you think about *why* you had done the wrong thing. He didn't judge you. And Tony's similar approach seems to have hit home.

Our Cornish friend takes out the device that carries the radio message. The words we listened to a few days ago blare across the field in front of the manor. "Please, whoever you are, whoever will hear this – come to Penzance. Our children have escaped to Tresco by boat. We need help. Everyone's gotten sick. Please, I beg you, save our children. Don't abandon them."

When the message is finished, Tony turns off his device again. "Someone had to come help the children. So Henry and I came here, even though it's one-hundred and fifty long years after this message was recorded."

Saul's face looks ashen. He has dropped the sword. The rope slips from his hand and his captive takes a few tentative steps back. The crowd in front of the porch parts to let Mara through, who pulls Andy away from the stairs.

"Can I hear that again?" the former manor leader whispers. "Please?"

Tony sits down next to Saul on the steps, and Leia cautiously joins them. Once again, he plays the message, which seems to have a hypnotic effect on the easterners. They seem baffled and mesmerized by it. Of course, we always believed someone would come for us from the Other Side, but they never did – until now. Some are brought to tears when they realize there is a very different side to their story. The Eldest approaches Tony and starts asking him all kinds of questions about the history of our ancestors.

My father and I shuffle forward to listen to the story again. Our visitor from Cornwall ends his narrative with an explanation for the book these people hold in such high esteem.

It is a diary, written by a scared and lonely child. In fact, it's the counterpart to the child's drawing made by Mary – the drawing that evolved on our temple walls into an illustration of our belief in salvation coming from far, far away.

"How old were those children?" Leia asks timidly.

"Six or seven," Tony replies, "but the oldest one was ten. He was the son of the man who recorded the message you listened to, and this ten-year-old reinvented himself. He decided that the world would be his stage, that he would become the hero he looked up to, teaching himself and others to tap into the force within themselves."

Leia's brother has joined our little interview circle. "So they had no parents," he says, overcome with grief. "They were all alone."

I shake my head. "Not all alone. At first they had the captain of their ship, but he probably got sick too, so he decided to sail back to Penzance before it would be too late. He appointed one of the children Bookkeeper before he left. He taught us there was great wisdom in the books."

And sadly enough, that wisdom hasn't been enough. The knowledge in our books was twisted and distorted; over the course of years, the books were disregarded in favor of folk tales told by ignorants, cast aside to be replaced by a religion that devolved into a system of constraint due to narrow-minded priests.

We should have assumed less and explored more. Maybe then, Toja wouldn't have run away, and my mother would have still been alive today.

In the flickering light of the torches now screwed into the ground to serve as illumination around the portico, Tony tells the easterners about *their* ancestors, their heroes.

It's strange, but I sense how some vital details in their legend are true. I realize that the stories about Annabelle, Luke and Leia are only fiction. However, that mysterious force flowing through everything like love supporting us from without *and* within is not a fabrication. It must be real.

How strange. All those years I spent visiting the temple weren't enough to make me feel this, but now, it's as if I can hear the hidden message in these stories from both sides, east and west, resounding in every last little word. And it fills my heart with joy.

"I found it, Grandpa Thomas," I whisper softly, looking up at the starry sky. "And I hope you have also found what *you* were looking for."

21.

WHEN WE get back to the central square in Newexter, Leia walks up to me and takes my hand. "Are you joining us at the village hall?" she asks. "Or will you sail back to the west with your father and uncle tonight?"

The army of Hope Harborers has done its duty. Uncle Nathan wants to sail back home as soon as possible to inform the people who stayed behind of everything that happened, so they'll continue straight on to the beach from here.

I clutch her hand. "I'll stay here tonight. Tony isn't leaving yet, either."

"You got a place to stay yet?"

I shoot her a cheeky look and start grinning. "Why? You got something to offer?"

Leia turns red. "You're doing it *again*," she prattles.

"What?" I ask innocently.

"Using that arrogant tone of voice and that fake charm!"

For just a second, her objection makes me pause, but then I grin even more widely. "As long as I can make you blush like that with my fake charm, I'm going to keep right on using it," I reply calmly.

She shrugs in frustration. "Well! I'll have to work on that, then," she huffs, but it doesn't sound unfriendly. Taking a step back, she adds: "Colin doesn't live at home anymore. He has a cottage together with Amy, because they're getting married. So you can sleep in his old room."

Married? So soon? But Colin is just as young as Leia. "And where do you live, exactly?" I inquire, suddenly feeling a bit insecure. Could she have a fiancé I don't know anything about?

"With my mom," she replies curtly. "So, uhm... I'm off to the village hall. Will you join us soon?"

I nod, staring after her as she enters the colorfully-decorated hall built of timber. Tony promised the most important people in the village to tell them more about their history in an evening session of sorts, but he also said we should discuss the future. What will happen now? What will the future have in store for the villagers of Newexter?

I linger outside, putting my hands in my pockets. My right hand suddenly hits something I'd completely forgotten about. Surprised, I pull out a partially flattened packet of cigarettes. It seems like a well-timed discovery – I could do with a smoke after all of tonight's excitement.

I pull the least flattened cigarette from the packet, dangle it between my lips and look around for something to light it with. Don't these people have torches on their street corners? Of course, there's the big fire in the middle of the square, but that seems like a bit too much of a risk.

"Over here," a voice unexpectedly calls out to me. It's coming from a bench hidden in a dark corner on the other side of the hall. "You need a light?"

I swivel around and walk in the direction of the shady corner. I'll be damned – it's *Saul* who addressed me. Next to him is his younger brother. Ben, I think his name was.

Saul is holding a piece of wood, one end still glowing from the fire. He's used it to light a cigarette of his own, or something like it, anyway. It smells weird and sweetish. I guess they smoke a very different kind of plant on this side of the Wall.

"Thanks," I mumble awkwardly, pressing the tip of the wood against my own cigarette. I personally have nothing against Saul – I mostly experienced him as being sick with desperation and sorrow – but I don't know what the rest of Newexter will think if I become smoking buddies with the antagonist of their whole tragedy.

"Can you tell us a bit more about the Fools?" Ben asks me curiously. "What do your people believe in? Is it really true that strangers have come from the Other Side to save us?"

I take a deep breath and squat down in front of them. "I don't think any of us still believe like we used to."

"So what do *you* believe in?" Ben persists.

Good question. What *do* I believe in? What have I learned from the stories about Annabelle and Luke?

"There is a force within you," I start out softly. "You can use that and develop it as long as you're open to it. But that doesn't mean you have to go it all alone."

Saul shoots me a dark, searching look. "Why not?" he mumbles.

I try to express in words what I felt inside, earlier this evening. "Because, at the same time, there's also a benevolent force watching *over* us. My people seek it in the sun and the flowers during spring and summer, in the colors of the red leaves in fall, and in the beauty of the glittering snow in winter. We invoke it at night by keeping the fires burning near the sea." I smile. "But I don't think we have to wait for it. It is already there, and it will always be with us."

We keep quiet after that and stare musingly at the fire in the middle of the square. Saul finishes his cigarette. Ben and he get up at the same time, and Saul nods at me briefly. "Thanks," he says. They disappear into the house belonging to the Eldest, who has temporarily adopted them. Not a bad move, in my opinion.

156

When my own cigarette is finished, I enter the village hall and surrender myself to whatever comes next.

"Walk with me?" Leia asks me later that evening, as we're rounding the corner and turning into the street where she lives with her mom. She tugs my hand and leads me to a little path behind her house, running up to a hill beyond a cluster of cottages.

"Where are we going?" I ask.

"I want to visit Father's grave, now that I'm back home."

The easterners bury their dead. They don't do final journeys or funeral barges. Graves seem to be the norm on the Other Side too, because Tony buried his friend Henry as well.

In a way, I am jealous of Leia. At least she knows where her dad's body is. On the other hand, I am also glad that my mother, Yorrick and my grandfather have sailed away. It was easier for me to let them go like that. Or at least, that's what I thought, but I realize now they will always be with me in some way.

Leia has decided to join us on the *Explorer* when we sail out. Some other easterners are also tagging along, which is great news, but to be honest I only care about the fact that I'll be seeing a lot more of Leia in the near future. Despite her sometimes infuriating behavior, she is actually a very warm and good person. We've agreed to make the trip to Hope Harbor together tomorrow. On our walk we'll be joined by some of the others as well as some workmen – tomorrow morning, a team from Newexter will go west, headed by the Eldest and his assistants. They are going to break down the Wall that's cutting Tresco in half, and the idea is to pave a new road that will connect Newexter and Hope Harbor.

Everything will change.

When we're standing by the grave and Leia puts a single flower on the stone marking the spot where her father is buried, she says in a faltering voice: "I still remember how he used to sing for me when it was my bedtime and I wouldn't go to sleep."

"That's what I remember about my mom, too," I say, surprised.

The pain is evident in her eyes when she looks at me. "I would have loved to hear him sing one more time. Now that the world has changed so much, he could have sung for my children. Played with them. Colin is devastated by Father's death, too."

"It's good the two of you have a place you can go to if you want to remember his life." I put an arm around her, and she warmly leans into me.

"That's true." She points at a few graves on the left. "Some other family members are buried here too, but I didn't know them well. My mother comes here a lot."

I take a step toward the grave next to her dad's, and stop breathing for a moment. A wave of dizziness and disbelief hits me. "Toja," I spell out the name on the headstone. "Who... who is she?"

"My grandmother," Leia replies, staring at me like I'm an idiot. "Why are you asking?"

"You mean your Foolish grandmother?"

Once again, she nods.

I let out an incredulous snicker. "Oh my Goddess." I close my eyes and rub my face for a moment. "Okay. Right."

"Walt, don't be weird. What's up?"

"*My* grandpa almost married *your* grandma."

She gapes at me like a seabass. "Huh?"

"Toja was my grandfather's first love. He never got over the fact that she left him. He talked about her so much. We even commemorated the day of her disappearance every year."

Leia lets her breath escape. "Did you know she was actually planning on returning to Hope Harbor? Together with my mom?"

"She was?"

"Yeah. She wrote about it. But she drowned before she could put her plan into action."

I plunk down on the ground next to the graves, shaking my head in bewilderment. "Our lives would have looked so much different if the Wall hadn't been there. If your 'Luke' hadn't taken off on his own with a few like-minded kids to start a commune on this side of the island. If we had known more about each other."

Leia squats down next to me. "Our lives *will* look very different. The Wall will be torn down. East and West will be reunited. Our island is no longer alone, isolated by waves as far as the eye can see. We *know* there is more, now."

"Are you brave enough to look that far?" I gently ask.

"Yes. I am now." Leia looks up at the night sky. "Because now I know I won't have to do it all by myself."

I stare down at her pale, beautiful face, barely illuminated by the light of the thin, crescent moon and the stars above. I take her hand and slowly caress her fingers with my thumb. And then, I lower my head and kiss her lips, trying to put everything I feel when I see her into that kiss: insecurity because she seems so unapproachable sometimes, warmth because I think she's a beautiful and wonderful girl, happiness because she survived Saul's dictatorship in one piece, and the butterflies I feel in my stomach when she looks at me.

To my utter surprise, Leia melts into my arms. She kisses me back with a passion that makes my cheeks flame with fire. A sweet scent of flowers fills my nostrils when her hair is ruffled by the breeze brushing the hilltop, and when she slips her arms around my neck, I moan inadvertently.

I slowly pull away. Clearly, I don't know the first thing about moral rules in a graveyard, but I have the distinct feeling we are breaking one right now.

Leia's breath is fast and shallow. "Walt, you are more charming than I gave you credit for," she says, a challenging smile on her face.

"Oh, thanks," I mumble huskily. "Uhm... I think."

"But you're still sleeping in Colin's room," she goes on to warn me, wagging her finger at me.

I bite back a laugh, slamming my first on my knee in mock-frustration. "What? Is that *all* I'm getting for pouring my heart and soul into that kiss? I meant to convince an Unbelieving girl to drag me into her bedroom within one day."

"I'm sorry, but it seems you have poor seduction skills."

"Plus, I raised an entire army for you so you could save your village."

"For which I am grateful. But you're still sleeping in Colin's room."

I try to grab her, but she dodges my attack. Giggling like a little schoolgirl, she jumps up and runs down the path.

I follow her and almost trip over my own feet in the dark, but I don't care one bit. There's a world waiting out there, Leia is coming with me, and that's good enough for me, for now. The lives of my cousin

and my grandfather are still intertwined with mine –
through my eyes, they will see how the World across
the Waters is doing.

Right now, I can't imagine a better future than
the one before me.

Epilogue

"STAND ASIDE please!"

Leia takes another step back with me when a workman from Newexter swings his sledgehammer and hits the Wall one more time, causing an avalanche of crumbling bricks and mortar to rain down.

Slowly but surely, they're making a hole that we will all fit through. This is the spot where they want to pave the way for easterners and westerners wanting to cross – the road that the Bookkeeper and the Eldest have decided to name the Scilly Way. They want to start roadworks as soon as possible, but I won't be there to witness it. I'll be on my way to Cornwall by then.

Behind me, Ben stoops and picks up a piece of brick. He stares at the tiny remnant of the Wall in contemplation and proceeds by putting it into his pants pocket.

When we crowd through the hole in the Wall and move into our forest, I purposely fall behind to draw level with Ben. "I didn't know you would join us too," I mumble.

Ben gives a shrug. "Well, now you do." He looks at me defensively.

"I wonder what you'll think of Hope Harbor," I continue with a friendly smile. "It's a beautiful place, you know."

"Yeah. Sounded like it, the way you told us about it the other night." Ben scowls at the dirt under our feet. "And I had to go. I couldn't have stayed."

I hesitate. "And Saul?"

"Saul couldn't leave."

"Why not?"

"He thought it was the easy way out. And he's not like that."

I nod. "Okay. I sort of get that."

We walk on in silence. The path through the trees seems so much narrower, now that more than a dozen people are trudging through the forest. We progress with difficulty. When Leia catches up with me a little bit later and offers me her drinking bag filled with water, I gladly accept. There's no wind under the trees, and we're all sweating like pigs.

"Is Ben coming with us on the *Explorer* too?" I ask her quietly.

She shakes her head. "He wanted to start all over again, he said. And what better place to have a fresh start than in a town where nobody knows you?"

Now that we're about to leave the island, I can't help but wonder when we'll return. I also want to start anew, but not necessarily in the World across the Waters. I want to know what Hope Harbor might look like now that we are going to change our ways.

When we finally get to town and I take the High Way to lead us straight down to the harbor so they'll see it before we reach it, the people from Newexter slow down to take in the breathtaking view. Sunlight is dancing on the sea, reflecting off the water in the distance, and the *Explorer* is bobbing on the waves like a white ship of wonder.

Leia squeezes my hand in excitement. "We're really going," she says with a quiver in her voice. "I can't believe we're going to get off the island."

I smile at her. "I'm happy you're looking forward to it so much."

Uncle Nathan meets us in the harbor to give the Eldest of Newexter a semi-formal reception. Behind him is Alisa, who breaks into a run when she sees me and gives me a bear hug. "Walt!" she screams out of breath. "You did it! And you're still alive!"

Chuckling, I try to pry myself loose from her smothering embrace. "I am. Isn't that great? And how have things been in town?"

I introduce Leia and Alisa to each other. Alisa gives me a wink that is so conspicuous I turn beet-red. Fortunately, she doesn't say anything about us showing up here together. Instead, she tells us that the Bookkeeper has decided to stay in Hope Harbor because most of the town is still in disorder. The majority of people are actually reluctant to sail to the other side – Alisa included – and the people who stay behind need their leader.

"I've already landed a job in the Peacekeeper's Office," she happily announces. "They needed more people, and I can study during my days off."

"What are they planning to do with Bram and Finn?" I inquire curiously.

"They'll be going to Newexter first thing tomorrow morning." Alisa casts her eyes over our group. "I was told by your uncle that the easterners would send one of their criminals to us so we could send their troublemakers to them. An exchange of bastards, so to speak."

I point at Ben discreetly. He's standing next to a mooring post, taking in his surroundings and the hustle and bustle of harbor life with eager eyes. "That's him."

"Him?" Alisa stares at him, mouth agape. "But... he's still so young."

"Not too young to make the wrong decisions," Leia comments a tad bitterly.

"Maybe you should familiarize him with Hope Harbor culture," I quickly suggest to Alisa. "He deserves a second chance."

Alisa nods. "I will."

My father spots us on the jetty and approaches us. "Did you bring your travel bag for the journey?" he asks Leia.

She pats the bag dangling from her shoulder. "I've packed some basic stuff."

"Good." He turns toward me. "I packed a bag for you too. We're leaving at twelve."

My gaze drifts to the clock tower. It is now a quarter to twelve, so we're right on time.

"I'll go and confer with the captain about the route," Tony informs us. He walks down the jetty and climbs onto the gangway.

Alisa grabs my shoulder and takes Leia's hand. "Will you come back really soon?" she asks, emotion threatening to crack her voice. "I may not want to sail out myself, but I do want to know *everything* about your trip to Cornwall."

"I don't know if we'll make it back soon, but we *will* be back," I promise. Leia nods in agreement.

"In the end, we do belong here on Tresco," she adds. "But this is the beginning, and we're going to see the rest of the world first."

When we cast off the ropes at the stroke of twelve, a large crowd had gathered on the docks to wish us a safe journey. Almost everybody in Hope Harbor has a family member, friend or acquaintance going on this adventure. We leave with fifty-five people on board – about as many as the *Annabelle* transported at the time.

For the first few minutes, I'm gripping the railing about as tightly as Leia does, because I still don't have sea legs and the sea is choppy. Once we've reached calmer waters, I let go and smile at the girl standing next to me.

"Well. We're on our way," I say redundantly.

"On our way to the promised land," she agrees.

Hand in hand, we stand and watch the island we grew up on from the stern. At first, the coastline fills the entire horizon, but the strong current and the wind in our sails soon take us further away. Tresco is getting smaller.

We stand and watch. We keep watching until the Island of Fools and Unbelievers is just a dot on the horizon. That's when we turn around and leave our island behind to go inside.

Check out these other books by Jen Minkman on Amazon!

Shadow of Time:
A YA/NA Paranormal
Romance set in Navajo
Nation

**Publication date:
December 2012**

The Boy From The
Woods:
A YA Romance, mixing
the best of contemporary
and paranormal

**Publication date:
December 2013**

Mailing List for New Releases:
http://eepurl.com/x1X9P

Acknowledgements

A big thank you to the people who helped me in the process of getting The Waves ready for publication! My fellow Dutchie and paranormal romance author Isabel Peters who helped me by proofreading the Dutch version of the story, my husband Nwel Saturay-Minkman and my sister Marije who proofread the English translation and had some really good advice; to all of you, thanks very much!

This is the first time I wrote a sequel to a book, and it was quite an adventure. Since The Island was a novella and (due to a 20,000 page limit) didn't touch on all the things I wanted to tell about Tresco, it didn't take me long to decide to return to the Island world one more time and write about Walt and his life on the other side of Tresco.
Once again, a big thank-you to my readers who kept telling me the Island deserved to be longer or needed a sequel. Without you, I might not have written The Waves, and I'm glad I did.

Jen Minkman.

http://www.jenminkman.nl
http://www.facebook.com/JenMinkmanYAParanormal
https://twitter.com/JenMinkman
http://jenminkman.blogspot.nl

Made in the USA
Charleston, SC
18 September 2014